About the Author

Arianne Richmonde is the *USA TODAY* bestselling author of the suspense novel, *Stolen Grace*, and the Pearl Series contemporary romance – *Shades of Pearl, Shadows of Pearl, Shimmers of Pearl, Pearl*, and *Belle Pearl*. Arianne is an American author who was raised in both the US and Europe and now lives in France with her husband and coterie of animals. She used to be an actress and the *Beautiful Chaos Series* is inspired by her past career—she is a huge fan of TV, film and theatre and loves nothing better than a great performance.

D1518253

Shining Star

(A Beautiful Chaos book)

by
ARIANNE RICHMONDE

This is the final book in the
Beautiful Chaos Trilogy:

Shooting Star

Falling Star

Shining Star

v

FEB   2017

We live in a rainbow of chaos.

Paul Cézanne

I FELT SAFE WITH LEO so close to me—
my only friend in the world right now, in this
airless, faceless room that was our jail. Leo was my
everything and had been for the past forty-eight
hours, although neither of us was exactly sure how
long we'd been prisoners here. Perhaps longer. My
mind so often wandered to Jake, pondering . . .
would he be thinking about me? Not just because I
wasn't there on set for the movie, but because he
really cared about *me*.

I asked myself what I would have done
without Leo, and it was only later when it was over
that I realized my mistake to have felt so happy to

have him here with me.

Our tongues searched each other in the darkness, our lips melting into one, long, sensuous kiss. To my surprise, it wasn't the frantic, carnal lust that Jake and I experienced together in the shower—when I so nearly lost my virginity—but gentle, loving, slow and tender. Here was Leo, this huge, muscle-bound guy adorned with homemade prison tattoos, able to show his sensitive side. I thought about what he'd said in the car before we'd been abducted, about wanting to have kids one day, and a family.

Leo was so much more caring than I imagined possible.

"I can't get close enough to you, baby," he groaned into my mouth.

I locked my arms around his neck and deepened the kiss, and in one quick movement he pulled my helpless body on top of his. I could feel his solid, thick erection trying to burst free from his boxer briefs. I was feeling almost delirious from lack of food, coupled with this unexpected desire for a man I had no idea I'd been attracted to. It was like there was a magnet pulling us together, and neither of us was able to break away.

He pulled my panties down over my butt, his hands so large that they cupped my buttocks entirely. He slipped what felt like his thumb inside me and I cried out.

"Fuck, you're tight," he said, the rest of his hand easing between the crack in my butt. Another rush of wetness gathered between my legs, hot and slick.

"That's what comes of being unopened goods, I guess," I mumbled, almost to myself as much as to him.

He froze. His thumb, which had been making delicious circling movements seconds earlier, now rested calmly inside me. I wanted him to continue so I writhed up and down, flexing my hips backwards and forwards.

"Unopened goods? You're not virgin, are you, Star?"

I was surprised, Leo being foreign, that he'd caught onto that expression. I kissed his earlobe, and threaded my fingers through his thick crop of hair, wishing I hadn't told him. By now, I was so bored of this virgin crap. Did it really make a difference, anyway? I was tired, hungry, and thought that if my crazy stepbrother had gone insane and was going to put a gun to my head, then Leo and I might as well enjoy life while we could. I now understood why in times of war people had more sex than usual. There was no way of knowing what would happen next. We were living on the edge.

"Oh baby," he said, taking his thumb out of me and kissing my hair, "you're my dream girl. So precious, my beautiful Star, so fucking unbelievable."

I nuzzled my nose against his warm cheek and felt the planes of his face; his high cheekbones, the stubbly edge of his square jaw, that wasn't too square—just softened enough to make him beautiful. In the darkness I had to rely on touch and sensation as I inhaled him—this man who was my anchor—the only person in the world who could take away the pain of my loneliness.

He whispered, "I'm not going to fuck you, Star. Not like this. Your first time needs to be special."

His reasoning was somehow shocking—I

hadn't expected this. Not at all. His rock-hard cock was the antithesis of his words.

"But—"

"You're half unconscious with hunger, baby—you need to be aware of choices you make. Choice like this is turning point in life."

"But . . ." I said again in a weak voice—not understanding what was happening—"that wasn't what you told me before; you said you'd take me to Heaven if I let you—"

"But if I'm to be your first, it changes everything. I want *all* of you, Star, not just sex. I could lick every inch of your divine body, but I know I wouldn't be able to control myself and I'd ravish you, probably too hard, too rough. I don't want to take advantage of you like this. Well, I do—of course I do—but it isn't right this way. Sleep on it, baby. If tomorrow you still want big, Ukraine brute like me, okay, I'll take you to the moon and back, and fuck you till you're seeing stars." He laughed. "But for now, you sleep on it."

"Okay," I agreed reluctantly, dazed and confused, my eyelids fluttering as I nodded off.

T HE CALL CAME AT four a.m. I rolled over in bed and felt someone there, wondering whom I'd brought home last night, then remembering my abstinence of late. Had I gone partying and forgotten what I'd done? Who *was* she?

But it was just Fierce, snoring away peacefully, his long heavy legs poking in my direction, his paws in my face. I grabbed my cell.

"Hello?"

"There's a ransom for Star," the voice said gravely, the second I picked up my cell. The husky

French accent on the other end of the line was unmistakable: Alexandre Chevalier. *Starr.* The rolling of the Rs.

"Fuck," I said. *So she and Leo hadn't run off together, after all?* "Who took them?" I asked, my adrenaline up, my heart pounding with fear, terrified for poor Star, feeling sick for Leo. I prayed that neither had been hurt. So many nutters out there. It was my fault; Star had needed a professional bodyguard, twenty-four-seven, and I'd fucked up.

"It was some foreign voice who called, phone untraceable. Sounded Eastern European. The FBI are now obviously involved—it's out of my hands."

My intestines felt like scrambled eggs. A chisel chipping away at my heart. I wanted to blame someone—anyone—but couldn't. I was the cause of this horror story, and what was unfolding was more dramatic, more heart-rending than any movie I'd ever made.

"You said you were tracing their cellphones," I said. "What did you find?"

"Friends, work related stuff. And the fact that

Star's calls were being tapped."

"No shit. That happened in England a few years ago. The tabloids were bugging celebrities' phones."

"It looks as if the tracker was her very own stepbrother, Travis."

"Shit! She mentioned once that they didn't get on. He was *spying* on her? You think he could be involved in the kidnapping?"

"It could be unrelated. But the fact that her calls were rubbed off, yet he was eavesdropping on her, does make it suspicious. Anyway, his cellphone has been tracked so his movements are being monitored by detectives."

"But you said that the person who's asking for a ransom has a foreign accent."

"Jake, I hate to say it, but this doesn't look good for your friend Leo."

I was trying to compute everything Alexandre had just said, but ignored his accusation about Leo. There were several dodgy Eastern European gangs in LA; just because Leo had a Russian/Ukrainian accent didn't make him guilty. "How much do they want?"

"Ten million dollars, cash, to be dropped off in a gym bag at a place of their choosing. I'm waiting for instructions."

"Do the kidnappers know the FBI's involved?" I'd seen enough thrillers to know how that one played out. Not cool for some dumb, overzealous FBI agent to bugger things up. I had Star's pretty face in my mind—a slash to the cheek, worse, a slash to the neck. Or what if they lost their marbles completely and killed her?

"No, of course they don't know about the FBI," Alexandre said, agitation thrumming in his vocal cords. "He/they/whoever—we still aren't sure who we're dealing with. Look, I have to go, but please keep this between us, Jake."

"Do the other producers know?"

"Brian knows. He's convinced that Leo is at the heart of this. A little suspicious, don't you think? The second Star's with him alone she goes missing? Leo's a strong guy—he could have protected her. Certainly has me wondering too."

"He . . . wouldn't, he . . . I don't think so, Alexandre. Really, I can't imagine he'd do something like that."

"Well, if you remember anything important, something that will give us a clue, call me." He hung up.

My head was reeling. Leo? A kidnapper? Fucking up his whole career opportunity for money? That wasn't like him at all. But then again, Brian had a point. Leo had been raised poor. Did time. Ten million dollars could buy him a lifetime's worth of anything he wanted. He'd often told me how he'd be happy to just be an artist. Perhaps that's all he wanted—to paint somewhere. Mexico maybe, or an island in the Caribbean. Tinkering around with a palette of oils in his hand, making home movies, drinking, and fucking pretty women. He'd always said that he didn't envy the red carpet aspect of my life. He wasn't ambitious the way I was; he was a pure artist, and it showed in his work.

I still couldn't get my head around it. Leo, a criminal? Well, yes, duh, he *was* a criminal. Just because he was my friend I'd never questioned the implications of it before. *He'd been in prison*! But killing a man in a temper for raping his sister was a far cry from kidnap.

I TOOK A COLD shower to wake myself up. It was as if I needed the shock of the chill to make myself understand I wasn't still sleeping: locked into some sort of nightmare. I don't know why, but I put on a suit. I rarely wore suits—nobody wears suits in LA—but it made me feel as if there was a modicum of control left in my life. I felt like crap on the inside; the least I could do was look good on the outside. No tie, though, that was going too far—this wasn't an award ceremony. I fixed myself a quick mug of coffee and called my assistant.

"Biff, how fast can you get here? You need to play chauffeur today."

"Sure, Jake. I was on my way over anyway, to drop off a script for you—I'll be with you in ten minutes."

I hung up, fetched Fierce's food, and measured two cups of dog kibble into his bowl. Seconds later, he came bounding in from the garden. It gave me pleasure to see such happiness; the smallest of gestures: food, a cuddle, a walk—for any of this I'd be rewarded with deep devotion and gratitude. I pitied anyone who had never known the love of an animal, and I thought of Star again. Her kindness to Fierce was one of the things that had made me fall in love with her. *Fall in love?* Really? These words had obviously been rumbling about in my subconscious and took me by surprise. Hard to admit to myself, but knowing that I could now lose Star forever forced me to look at my life—and her—in a new way.

I placed Fierce's bowl on the floor. He sat politely waiting for the command. "Good boy!" I said, clapping my hands. "And eat up, Fierce, you've got a job to do today."

I went back upstairs, into Star's bedroom. Ever since she had been living with me I referred to it that way. Her things were still scattered around. "Respect For Acting" by Uta Hagen—one of those Method books—was lying on her bedside table, along with her e-reader.

We'd spent hours discussing her craft, and the more I got to know her, the more I understood how serious she was about her profession. She wasn't just a movie star; she was an *actress*. A consummate professional. She'd talked about the exercises in this book. The "Three Entrances" for instance. When you came onto the set or onstage, where were you coming from? Had you lost your keys? Were you thirsty? Had you just broken up with your boyfriend? It was no good, she explained to me, just hitting your mark, or getting on that stage—you had to know *why* you were there and bring your character's "baggage" and history with you to every scene.

"I'm not doing this for the money, Jake," she told me one night at dinner. "I'm acting for free. What am I getting paid all these millions for? The bullshit that comes with it. The meetings, the politics, the waiting in my trailer between takes. The acting I do for free."

I was impressed. Nobody had ever said anything like that to me before. Least of all the actresses I'd hung out with.

Then Star whispered in my ear, "I sort of stole 'the acting I do for free' line from Michael Caine," she admitted, "one of the greatest actors out there, because what he said suits me perfectly. He played my grandfather once, and believe me, that man can act his way out of a paper bag."

I'd noticed something about Star and her world. All these movie greats were her buddies, calling her for a chat, e-mailing or texting her. They respected her talent. They adored her. I too had fallen under her spell.

And now she'd been fucking well kidnapped! And I was to blame.

I opened her closet and my nose prickled, my eyes threatening to well up at the sight of all her beautiful clothes, bringing back vivid memories. Dinners, the skimpy little skirt she wore when we made out on the couch, the tiny bikini she strutted about the house in—that she knew was killing me—was lying on the floor next to a pair of high black shoes. Those she'd worn to the read-through. I grabbed them and one of her dresses; one she'd worn recently that I knew hadn't been dry-cleaned. Star was "green," insisted upon eco-friendly dry cleaners so her skin wouldn't be "laced with carcinogenic toxins," so that one still hadn't been sent out.

I heard the doorbell and knew it was Biff.

Good, we needed to get going. I then rushed to my bathroom and fished a T-shirt out of the laundry basket. Luckily, I'd given the cleaner an extra day off, and a T-shirt I'd lent Leo to go running in was still dirty. "Fierce?" I shouted. "Are you ready, boy?" I dashed downstairs, my faithful dog bounding after me. Biff was there—another faithful friend. She was dressed in army fatigues and boots, and her trademark rectangular black glasses—she almost looked like she was ready for combat.

3. Star

I AWOKE WITH A JOLT, an idea springing my eyes wide open. It was early, maybe four or five a.m. judging from the pale, diffused light coming through the window.

I nudged Leo. "Leo, the tin cans! We can pile them up—give us extra height to stand on. Maybe get into the space above the false ceiling." I'd thought of also using the cans to smash the triple-glazed windows, but was sure it would be useless. Even if we managed to crack the glass, which was extremely unlikely, we were so high up. Scream out? There were no buildings as high as this, nobody would hear us. Wave a flag? We didn't have anything to wave except my bra. Jump? Yeah, right. In any case, the thickness of the glass made all these scenarios a fantasy. Although I supposed there wasn't any harm in trying.

Leo groaned, his arms enveloping my body once again. It all came back to me; we had been on the brink of having sex last night, but now all I could concentrate on was escaping. Priority number one.

"Where are we?" Leo mumbled, speaking in his sleep, his arms traveling down my back and wrapping around my waist.

"In the Garden of Eden," I replied sarcastically. "Wake up, Leo, we have to find a way outta here."

He opened his dark brown eyes, one, then the other—his long lashes creating shadows on his face. Then he blinked. "It's true," he said. "I really am in Garden of Eden—your face is Paradise, baby."

"It'll be paradise when we get the fuck out of here," I said, trying to slip away. He wasn't as agitated as I was about being locked up, because getting out of this place was consuming my every thought. He'd eaten, I hadn't. Perhaps having been in prison he could adjust. I couldn't. I struggled against him.

But he wouldn't let me go and clutched me tighter to him, his soft skin against my bare body, the gorgeous smell of him tempting me to remain in the comfort of his arms all day. I sighed. "Look, if we see there's no way, we can come back to bed. Is that a deal?"

He winked at me. "Deal."

I sprinted to the bathroom, peed, washed, brushed my teeth, rinsed and spat, glugged down some tap water, all in record time, and set upon the tins, gathering them up.

"What's that noise?" Leo said.

I was making such a clatter, coupled with the thumping of my racing, excited heart at the possibility of escape, I couldn't hear.

"Shush," he said. "Is someone coming?"

I froze my movements and perked up my ears, which had become keen to the tiniest sound. Even the low buzz of the florescent strip-light had begun to sound like a jet. Although, right now, the light was off.

Footsteps. Male footsteps.

Leo and I looked at each other, then back to the door with no handle.

It was terrifying not knowing what would happen next. I was now starring in my very own Hitchcock movie. Lead role. I held my breath for as long as I could, fearful someone might hear me, but then sipped in as much air as possible as I thought I'd faint. Leo pulled me up from the floor, not making a sound, and held me close against his chest. I felt his heartbeat thrum against my semi-nudity; I was exposed and glad to have him as my protector, but through his silence, I could feel his fear too.

The door unlocking seemed as if it was happening in slow motion; every click, every clatter, every turn was like an eternity, yet it was also over in a second. Time was playing tricks with my head.

I clasped Leo, squeezing my arms around his strong body, resting my head against his chest.

The door swung open. I was expecting Travis, but a skinny, wiry man with a haggard, weathered face walked in. His sleeves were rolled up and he sported the same type of smudgy tattoos as Leo. The man's eyes were pinned and hollow as he took me in. I pressed my chest against Leo's frame to hide my nakedness.

Leo shouted at this man in his native language. The man hadn't even spoken but Leo was talking to him like he knew him.

Leo *knew* him?

I felt sick to my stomach—sped-up details flashed before me. The car drive. The restaurant parking lot. My house. Blacking out.

Had I been set up?

By *Leo*?

Leo—and whoever this man was—were in it together. Leo had orchestrated my abduction. That's why having sex with me earlier was more important to him than escaping, that's why he had seemed so nonchalant about us being locked up! He had hardly questioned it. Now I knew why. I couldn't speak. I was struck dumb.

The man was screaming at Leo to let me go. I couldn't understand a word but I could tell by his gestures.

It finally dawned on me.

I'd been kidnapped. I was their money prize and they were fighting over me.

I let out a high-pitched curdling scream, yodeling at the top of my lungs. Maybe now that the door was ajar my sound would travel and somebody in the building would hear me.

Leo pressed his hand over my mouth. "Baby, please, I don't want him to hurt you."

Baby? Leo had kidnapped me and was calling me *baby*?

I started to struggle from his grip, but it was useless. Even at the best of times I would have gotten nowhere as Leo was a hundred times stronger than me, but I was also weak, undernourished. And apparently Leo was determined to get what he wanted:

Me.

But for all the wrong reasons.

Leo held me close, continuing to shout at the wiry Russian man: his partner in crime.

I cried out, clawing at Leo's torso with my nails, begging him to explain, "You bastard, who the hell *are* you?" but his large hand over my mouth muffled my cries. I had never felt so betrayed in my life, but at the same time, it dawned on me that I didn't want him to release me. It was as if I had Stockholm Syndrome—in love with my captor. I felt that I needed him even though I hated him. And right now, I really did. Both. Need him and hate him at the same time.

I held onto Leo tighter and terrified myself by my actions: I started kissing his hand. Over, and over. I raised my eyes to him, pleading. Pleading for him to keep me safe with him. To not deliver me to this cavernous-eyed man, whose pockmarked face was the personification of evil. His fine hair was slicked back into a greasy ponytail, his window's peak making him look like the Devil himself.

He took several steps closer, speaking as he walked. Calmer now, but even more deadly. I clung onto Leo.

"I'm so sorry, baby," Leo said. "I can't believe this has happened. I thought he was dead." He took his hand away from my mouth.

"Who the hell *is* he?" I gasped, then gulped down a breath of air.

"My uncle," he said with a tone of apology.

A myriad of images came to my mind. Leo in prison. His uncle orchestrating his escape. Leo coming to London to pay back his debt by "working" for him. Then film school where he was a star pupil, winning first prize to work with Jake. Jake trusting him, loving his work. Leo telling me in the car that, in so many words, his uncle meant nothing to him.

This soul-defying man—his uncle—lurched forward and tried to take my hand. Leo had no alternative but to let me go, stepping in front of me and acting as a buffer between us. Leo pushed me backwards, away from the sweaty grasp of my enemy, and I stumbled, pathetically covering my upper body with my hands. I stood, shivering in my underwear, too stunned to run.

They were screaming at each other in Russian. Ukrainian? Whatever, it was heated. I looked down at the floor and saw one of the tin cans that had rolled its way over, not far from me. I eyed the Heinz Baked Beans longingly, but at the same time, I didn't want to let my gaze stray from Leo. The second I could, I stuck out my foot and hooked the can towards me the way soccer players do, bent down and snatched it up, clenching it in my grasp, then backed myself up so I was against the wall.

I shot a glance at the door as I heard it creak, but nobody was there. I looked back at Leo and his uncle. I held onto the baked beans for dear life—literally—my only weapon to protect myself.

The man lunged at Leo, his right fist hooking him on the jawline—this man looked scrawny but was tough, steely and mean. The twisted look on his face, the tight lips, his brawny clenched muscles said it all. More swearing and cursing in this language I didn't understand. Leo stood tall and jumped in the air, landing a sort of Kung Fu kick in the abdomen of his adversary, and his uncle tottered backwards, clenching his solar plexus in pain. But this guy was trained, I could tell. He quickly rolled in a somersault, and taking advantage of Leo's height and his own small build, he hooked his foot around Leo's left ankle, taking him off balance and forcing him to topple to the ground. I could see he wanted to kill his nephew.

The idea of anything happening to Leo filled me with horror. I wanted to bash this man on the head with the tin can but couldn't get anywhere close. The two were both now on the floor, Leo only in his boxer briefs, but the uncle in a pair of heavy army boots, fatigues, and a black shirt, rolled up at the sleeves.

I watched them wrestle on the floor. Leo got in a hard punch on the uncle's nose and he cried out, but he grabbed Leo's thick hair and pulled his face toward him, uttering threats and curses. Leo took his shirt collar in his hands, his fists crossed, pulling the shirt collar together tightly so the fabric itself was strangling him, the man's windpipe gasping against Leo's closed fists, his Adam's apple bobbing up and down, squelched against the pressure being exerted on his throat. And that's when I heard him wheeze, speaking English for the first time:

"Travis, you fuck. Travis, help me!"

Travis? Travis, my brother? So he was a part of this, after all?

I glanced at the door, but still, nobody seemed to be there, so I ran at Leo's uncle, skidding down on my knees so I was at ground level. I started to pound his head with the tin can. I closed my eyes so I couldn't see what I was doing but heard a crack. The skull? I felt something spray me in the face and for a second I thought it was warm water, but when I opened my eyes my body was splattered with blood. Horrified by what I had done, I dropped the baked beans. I dry-retched, always thinking how ridiculous it is in movies people want to vomit at times like this, but that's exactly what my body tried to do, but I had no food inside my stomach to let that happen. I was disgusted with myself, with all the blood. I couldn't believe what I'd just done. The man was barely alive, gasping for air, but then he seemed to go still.

Leo locked his eyes with mine. "He was threatening to kill you, baby, don't for second feel bad. This piece of shit will do world favor by checking out for good."

My mouth hung open—no words came out. A tear slid down my cheek.

"Just a bit of blood, baby. I took the air out of him. I did it, not you."

He was trying to make me feel better; like I was innocent, like I hadn't done a thing. But I could see inside the depths of my soul and I saw a killer, a woman who would *kill* for her man, even if he was a murderer. That's when I understood how deep our bond was, and it appalled me.

"I think I love you, Star," Leo uttered, a faint smile flickering on his lips. "I love you, baby." And he winked at me. "You and me? We're forever. You love me, don't you? You know I want to marry you now, don't you?"

The door suddenly swung wide open. It was Travis, standing there with a gun in his hand.

Leo stood up, facing me, his back to the door, but he started to turn to see who had entered. He had just professed his love like we were Bonnie and Clyde, like this was a part of who we were. But I didn't *know* who he was. I didn't know who *I* was either—this alien person—me—who was capable of spilling blood. Then it dawned on me: I was like my character, Skye. I had become her. Yet I still didn't know what the hell was going on. But before I had a chance to ask—before I even had a chance to scream, or warn Leo that Travis had a gun in his hand—a shot rang through the room.

Another spray of blood as Leo sprang

backwards—literally—like some force had propelled him into the air and punched him back down. Travis had shot him, and the bullet had pierced right through . . .

His heart was pouring blood.

I heard a scream, so loud it deafened my ears.

I watched a girl break down, her half naked, bloody body fling itself on this man she loved, tears streaming from her eyes. I observed this girl as if I were hovering in the air, like I was floating above the scene.

Leo lay there, motionless; scarlet liquid—so bright it shone—gurgling from his body like a babbling brook. The girl covered her body over his, weeping hysterically, sucked into a black hole of nothingness.

Then I realized . . .

That girl was me.

PRODUCTION
Shining Star

DIRECTOR
. bke Wild

DATE
. Ine

SCENE
Star's house

TAKE
4

CAMERA
. bke Wild

I RANG THE BELL at the entrance of Star's home, by the imposing, black, wrought iron gates of her Spanish colonial in Hancock Park, while Biff waited for me in the car.

Funny, I would never have pegged Star as the type to own a house in this neighborhood. The people here are conservative with old money. Most celebrities prefer Beverly Hills, Bel Air, or Malibu. So Star making this her number one choice, when she could have lived anywhere at all, surprised me. And not. The more I knew Star, the more I realized I'd misjudged her. She was not some fame-junkie celeb. She was a serious actress who wanted a normal life, who had taken a couple of wrong turns, nothing more, and who—in her heart—was genuine. The real deal.

I had purposefully parked my car on the street so Fierce and I could go by foot. By paw. He was already sniffing excitedly. I had my Leo-smelling T-shirt in one jacket pocket, while holding onto my dog's leash, and draped over the crook of my other elbow, was Star's dress.

My idea was a long shot. Crazy, really. But Fierce could find a ball in the dark, even if you threw it a hundred yards. He had an uncanny sense of smell. His breed was loyal, too. Designed to pin down a lion, keep it at bay until his master arrived. That's how valiant the Rhodesian Ridgeback breed is. But the chance of Fierce sniffing down Star and Leo was slim. I must have seemed ridiculous. Like some silly amateur sleuth. Still, by this point I was willing to try anything.

A voice spoke out from the intercom. A woman with a Hispanic accent. "Yes?"

"Jake Wild here."

"Miss Davis is not at home. It is very early, Mr. Wild."

I looked at my watch. Shit, it was six a.m. Yes, very rude and ill-mannered to barge in on someone so early in the morning. But what was I supposed to do? Sit around at home and wait for news?

Another voice came through the intercom. "Jake? It's Janice. Is everything okay? Come on in." She buzzed the gates open.

Fierce and I slipped through the gates and I pulled out the T-shirt so he could have another sniff. They'd said that Star and Leo allegedly left in her Porsche, which Janice had told me was housed in Star's garage, which meant they had stopped at her house to pick it up at the end of the day's shoot. I figured—unless Leo had been lying—that he would have only visited this house once, so his scent would give me more of a clue than Star's as to where they went afterwards. A bit dumb, really, hardly likely that Fierce could track them after they'd got into her car—they hadn't been on foot. I was pulling at straws but it made me feel better about myself. I had to do *something*. I was still confused as hell. Was Leo guilty, or innocent? At this point, it hardly even mattered anymore—all I cared about was Star's safety and finding her unharmed.

Fierce pulled at the leash, but in the middle of the driveway he stopped in his tracks, sniffing in zigzags, but not venturing far. The scent ended here. In this spot. I shoved Star's dress under his nose and then he pulled me all over the place: into the garden, then round to the front steps of the entrance, then back, then towards the garage. In short, everywhere. Normal—she lived here. Which made me wonder; it didn't seem as if Leo had even entered the house. Unless Star had gone into her garage alone to get the Porsche, and brought it around to this spot in the driveway.

It was obvious that the missing Porsche was a ruse. Whoever abducted them wanted to make it look as if they'd gone off somewhere together. Perhaps that was why the kidnapper had taken their passports too. Or maybe just to maintain control; make sure they wouldn't leave the country if they managed to escape. The kidnapper was clever; a planner.

Janice opened the door and stood there in a dressing gown. I could hear the TV going in the background, or the radio—she had obviously hardly slept. Her wild red hair hung over her puffy eyes. "What the heck are you doing here so early?" She stifled a yawn.

"Sorry, Janice, I didn't realize anyone other than the maid would be here, but true, it's not very polite to make house visits at dawn. Still, right now 'polite' isn't very relevant, is it?"

She forced a limp smile. "Slept over. Didn't go home. Conked out watching TV. Just wanted to be closer to Star, you know."

I nodded. "I thought her house was undergoing renovation?"

"They took the scaffolding away yesterday, along with the crime scene tape."

"They put tape here? I thought they only did that with dead bodies."

"They were here dusting for fingerprints. Or trying to. I don't think they found anything."

"How do you know they didn't find anything?"

"A hunch, I guess. I got talking to one of the cops and they didn't seem to have any leads. Excuse me, how rude of me. Come in and have some coffee."

"You don't mind dogs?"

"I love dogs. May I?" she said, leaning down to pet Fierce's head.

"His name's Fierce."

She laughed and made cooing noises. "But you're not fierce at all, are you sweetie?"

I followed her through the hallway to the kitchen, Fierce's nails clicking on the cool, terracotta tiles. The hallway was replete with framed photos of Star on set, with all her famous co-stars over the years. I tried to imagine the stills of *Skye's The Limit* on these walls too. Creative visualization—a trick to make the future happen the way you want it to. There was a newspaper splayed open on a marble table with the headline: STAR DAVIS AND PLAYBOY LOVER STILL MISSING. My stomach took a dip.

I could smell coffee brewing and was grateful for Janice's hospitality. Yet not a bloody clue as to what I expected to find out. Star and Leo had been abducted. From her house. In her driveway. Which meant someone had been waiting for them. No shit, Sherlock!

So now what?

5.
Star

I LUNGED AT MY brother. Viciously. I didn't care that he had a smoking gun in his hand. I didn't, in that second, even care if he killed me too.

"You monster!" I yelled, crashing into him and pummeling his chest, my fists pounding frantically at his shoulders, neck, head—anywhere they landed.

But he stood there, not bothering to stop me, his freckled face even paler than usual, sweat dripping from his brow, stunned, immovable, staring in shock at Leo's dead body. He handed me the gun, not because he wanted to, but because his fingers just couldn't hold on any longer and were giving way.

"Is he dead too?" he muttered.

"Of course he's dead, asshole! You put a bullet through his heart."

"Not him. Boris. Is Boris dead?"

"Boris? He's your buddy?"

"We were . . . partners." Travis was in a daze. An automaton. He stayed rooted to the spot, still unable to budge. He wasn't even looking at me— just straight ahead, his gaze unfocused. I put the loaded gun gently on the floor, and then kicked it away so it slid to the other side of the room. I could have held onto it, but I didn't dare. Our dad had taught us how to shoot, how to defend ourselves, and Travis was stronger than me. I was too weak to do a "citizen's arrest" – too, shaky. And a voice inside my head told me that holding a gun to my brother was a bad idea. I might be tempted to pull the trigger.

"You and this guy Boris were working together? To kidnap me? To lock me in this room? *With no fucking food?*"

Travis nodded.

"And Leo? Was he in on it too?"

He shook his head and whispered, "No."

Relief surged through my body like a color. The color blue. As if all the evil had been cleansed with a clean sea-blue, washing away the pain, at least for a nanosecond. Leo had not betrayed me after all.

I shook my brother, my nails tearing into his jacket. "How did you meet this guy Boris?"

"He came to the house," he mumbled in a low monotone, "looking for Leo. He'd heard about the movie—knew that his nephew was working with you on *Skye's The Limit*. We started talking."

'The' house was *my* old house—the house I gave to Travis. To be nice. To get him out of my hair. To appease him. Keep him happy and leave me alone. But it hadn't worked. He wanted more. Always *more*. And now he had ruined my life and taken away someone else's: Leo's.

"You and Boris plotted together to kidnap me?"

He nodded again. "I'm sorry, Star. No one was meant to get hurt. I panicked, I—"

"Put your hands in the air where we can see them!"

I had been so focused on my brother that I hadn't heard the commotion—the swarm of buzzing bees—dark blue outfits, gold badges—the LAPD swat team bursting through the door, their loaded guns pointed in every direction. Two huge men grappled Travis from behind and pinned him facedown on the floor. They handcuffed him, wrists behind his back. Two others rushed over to Leo and his uncle, stepping around the pools of blood to take their pulses, to see if there was life coming from the mess on the floor. Another took me by the arm, at this point not knowing if I was guilty or innocent. Or so I guessed.

"Star Davis?"

"That's me," I croaked. "Please, I need to say goodbye." I yanked myself away from the officer's grip and dashed towards Leo.

"I'm sorry ma'am, this is a crime scene, step back from the—"

At that point, I heard that girl scream again, a new surge of sobbing shaking her body, ripping through every fiber of her being. A demented, deranged spirit that had wound its way deep, deep into her psyche.

And wouldn't let go.

WHEN I OPENED MY EYES I was in a white room. But then I crushed my lids closed again, remembering that I was still alive, and that the only thing that gave me reprieve from the nightmare of life . . . was sleep. I felt a hazy whir in my head and let myself fall away again.

Sleep . . . my escape.

Not long later, I cracked my eyes open once more, and my new prison came into focus, little by little. A large window, daylight diffused by a gauzy white curtain but with bars so you couldn't get out. A poster on the wall, which at first I thought was a painting. White bedclothes, starched crisply clean.

There was an empty feeling in the pit of my stomach, which I took to be hunger, but then realized was a gouge so deep that no amount of food could fill it. Only misery.

Leo is dead.

The only thing that could help me, I thought,

was to get back to work. I needed to work. Return to the set.

I had to get out of here. I raised my body forward, but a force stopped me like an invisible hand punching me backwards. I looked down and saw a thick metal mesh restraint at my waist, holding me to the bed.

What? I'm in a fucking straitjacket?

That's when I understood.

A straitjacket, or whatever this is, is for dangerous people, not movie stars. I really am in prison . . . because I killed a man.

I racked my brains, back to the moment when the cops arrived: two dead men, Travis, and me. The gun was on the floor. *Maybe they think I shot Leo too? Travis is a good liar.*

I retraced my fragmented memory. I remembered running to Leo, wanting to say goodbye, and that's the last I could recall. Did they sedate me? Did a paramedic give me a shot? Did they arrest me?

Because what the hell am I doing here restrained?

I felt the confines of my new outfit. The vest connected to a metal rail, either side. My fingers walked along the cold stainless steel, shooting signals to my brain, sending shivers bouncing along my spine. I tried to free myself once more by lurching forward, but the straps dug into my chest.

Where am I?

"BABY, IT'S ME."

I open my eyes. A figure is standing over me. Looming. Large. A male nurse? But he's so close; his breath on my face, his lips hovering over mine. Am I dreaming? I shake my head and even pinch myself because I cannot believe my vision: Leo leaning over my hospital bed! He traces his fingers along my jawline.

"But you're dead!" I exclaim, thinking I'm seeing a ghost, not a real live person. "My brother shot you *dead*."

His lips are still so close to mine. I can smell his minty breath. And apricots. Mint and apricots. "He shot me in arm, that's why there was so much blood. The pain knocked me out cold. You were so hysterical they took you off, but I didn't get taken to ambulance in body-bag, baby. They put me on *stretcher* and took me to hospital, dressed my wound, and here I am. Lucky my big biceps got in way—bullet missed my heart. Shot right through my ugly-ass tattoo." He laughs joyously and my eyes fill with tears of happiness. Gratitude. Relief. *Is this really true?*

"I missed you so much," I whisper. "I thought you were dead. I wasn't sure how I could carry on anymore." I try to sit up but my straitjacket thing won't give me more than a few inches leeway.

"Let's get you out of vicious contraption."

"Where am I?" I ask. "Am I in jail? For killing your uncle?"

Leo laughs. "You didn't kill him, I did. I bribed nurse to let me in. Like security hospital. Had to sneak in," he breaths into my mouth while undoing the straps. "We have unfinished business, Star."

"I know," I say, and I let my lips touch his. My heart's racing. I'm alive again, not the dead zombie I felt like earlier.

His tongue searches its way into my mouth,

coaxing mine, and I let it in, moaning as we kiss. I'd almost forgotten how sweet he is, even though it has only been twelve hours, but it already feels like a lifetime. I grab his good arm, the one that hasn't been bandaged, and pull him even closer.

I take a breather from the kiss and mumble into his mouth, "All I could think of was never seeing you again. Never kissing you again, of having been a fool not to have let you break my virginity—"

"I'm here, baby, I'm here—no time to lose now." He stands up straight then slips himself onto the bed. "No room side by side for big brute like me. You on top, yeah?"

He maneuvers me so I am lying on top of him. He raises his arms, wincing with pain as he does so. "Help me take T-shirt off." I slip the T-shirt over his chest and head, with a sigh. How I missed his body! Those crazy tattoos that are a part of his tumultuous past, that follow the lean, ripped curves of his pecs and his abdomen—the tattoos that tell his dark story.

I burrow my nose into his neck and inhale his scent. Manly. Rough, a faint smell of sweat, mixed with his natural woody smell. Sun-warmed-smelling skin. "We understand each other," I whisper, trailing kisses all over him. "You and me. We have a bad side."

"Yeah, but we're so good together. Two goods can't make bad, baby." Leo kisses me again, but not softly this time. He takes my face in his hands, the tips of his fingers tugging gently on my hair, and he consumes my mouth, his tongue ravishing and tangling with mine, licking and sucking. I sense that familiar beat between my thighs: the beat of sexual desire. I open my legs. All I'm wearing are my panties and a sort of light hospital gown.

"This time, Star, I'm going to fuck you. Are you ready for that step?" I nod. "I want you, baby, more than I've wanted anything in my life," he tells me. He rolls my panties down, his hands caressing my ass—then squeezes it, sending signals directly to my clit, which begins to throb with anticipation. He glides his hands down my thighs, down my calves, his thumbs hooked into my panties. I cross my ankles over and flick them away, and they land on the floor. Leo rips off my gown in one, ravenous tug.

"Yes," I moan. "Please, Leo, don't go easy on me—fuck me like you mean it." I feel his huge erection pressed against my stomach, hard as an iron rod, straining against his jeans. "Take those off," I pant.

He grapples with his jeans, and I help him. They land on the floor with a thud, along with his boxer briefs. He's naked, and I gasp.

He licks his lips and stares into my eyes—lust his weapon. "You wanna suck my cock?"

Oh God, yes. He's holding his huge, thick cock in his hand, and I marvel at the size. It's perfect: a whopping great enormous dick with a soft wide crest that I can't wait to wrap my lips around. I open my mouth in preparation, but he slides down the bed under me and grabs my behind, pulling my hips so my crotch is on top of his face. He runs his nose along my inner thigh, inhaling deeply as if he's smelling a bouquet of roses, and trails feathery kisses along my sensitive skin.

"You smell fucking incredible." He nips me lightly. "Your skin so soft, Star. I wanted to eat your pussy so bad, baby. All that time we were locked up? What waste. Could have been fucking whole time."

"I know," I gasp, as his head presses between my thighs—I'm practically sitting on him. I bring myself up to my knees so I don't crush his face.

"This. Is. Mine. Do you understand, Star? This tight, hot, little virgin pussy belongs. To. Me. And once we've fucked, there's no turning back. It's you and me forever, babe. I'm possessive, and I don't share my treasure." His large hands cup my butt and he brings my hips even closer to his mouth, licking in great sweeps along my slit. I cry out.

"I killed for you, Star, and I'd do it all over again."

"I know," I breathe. *This man loves me so much, he killed for me.*

"Sweeter than candy, baby," he mumbles, dipping his tongue inside me, his fingers playing with my peaked nipples. "You're my dream girl. I love you, Star."

My heart's pounding with fear and excitement. Excitement because he just told me he loves me. Fear because he's big and I know when he does fuck me it's going to hurt. He starts to flicker his tongue on my clit really fast, and then sucks all of me into his mouth in a vacuum, moaning as he does it. Then he flicks his tongue back and forth again, growling—literally growling. He's carnal, animalistic. Devouring me. There's no finesse, just a wild beast who wants me all to himself.

I'm soaked. My very own juices, just for Leo. If he keeps this up I'll come soon. But I don't want to come this way. This is my first time and I want it to be with him inside me.

Gripping his shoulders, I slide down his body. He takes my pebbled nipple in his mouth and sucks greedily. The tingling sensation is echoed deep inside me, and when he takes my other nipple softly between his teeth, I start trembling. The head of his erection is poised at my slick-wet opening, and I can't hold out a second longer. Being on top means I can control the pace. I let him slip in, his soft crown easing me open. The sensation is incredible. He groans.

I hear myself whimper. "Oh my God!" We stare into each other's eyes, not breaking contact for a second.

"Doesn't it feel great?" he says, his hands in my hair. "And after you come, you'll want more. You said you had addiction before? Just you wait, Star, you'll get addicted to this. Addicted to my hard cock." On those words he slams himself into me, pulling my butt down hard on him, impaling my virginity with no mercy. I cry out, but surprisingly not in pain, but relief. Finally it's over—this precious chastity I've been holding as my trump card all these years. I have chosen Leo and it feels amazing.

He holds me tightly against his body, his huge cock stretching me open, filling me. Leo groans again. "Fuck you feel incredible. So tight. So wet. Are you alright, baby? Does it hurt?"

"A bit." It does hurt but it's a sweet sharp pain that I welcome. I ease up slowly, using Leo's shoulders as leverage, my tongue in his mouth. This time it's me that comes crashing back down on him, spearing myself with his hardness, entering even deeper than before.

He groans again and plays with my nipples between his thumb and forefinger. All of me is connected. "You're an angel," he moans into my lips. "A fucking goddess. You were made to be mine."

I rise up again and a rhythm gets established. Each time I come back down I grow more accustomed to his size; this alien thing inside my body, which begins to feel so natural.

Up and down, over and over. But when I'm down again I discover a new delicious thrill: making little circular movements, discovering that my clit gets a massage on his firm abdomen. Every. Time. I'm getting double the pleasure in two places. I lie pressed on top of him, rocking back and forth, back and forth, each time rubbing my swollen nub against him as the movements of his cock stroke me deep inside. My eyes roll back in ecstasy. *Yeah, I could get addicted to this.*

"Keep fucking me, baby, you're the best." His hands are cupping my butt, bringing me hard down on him every time his hips rise to meet me. I can feel blood rush to my groin, and Leo keeps pounding into me relentlessly from his position underneath. Hard. Cleaving into me, through me, some part of him slapping over and over against my clit. He continues thrusting back and forth, and

I feel it coming; a crescendo of nerves all gathering in the center of my body. I'm quivering. Me and Leo. Leo and me. As one. Our groins one living being, locked together in harmony. I collapse on top of him—his last plunge sending my body into a detonating, exploding wreck. Leo has ripped an orgasm clean out of me as if he owned it.

"I'm coming, Leo." Tears are pouring out of my eyes, and he cries out as his scorching climax shoots out of him and into me; his vessel of love.

"Your orgasms are mine, baby. All mine. And mine are yours. We're one now."

'**W**E INTERRUPT THIS story to bring you breaking news concerning the actress, Star Davis. A Twitter post today started a media frenzy, in what can only be described as the most talked-about news to date concerning the star. We are here live, outside this abandoned building in Downtown LA. Ms. Davis was discovered during the early hours this morning, just a few hours ago, locked up in a room on the twenty-second floor, unable to escape. She was the victim of a kidnapping, alongside her alleged lover, Leo Turgenev, who had been working with her in the movie production of Skye's The Limit, directed by Jake Wild.

"Leo Turgenev and another Ukrainian man, believed to be a relative of his, have been found dead at the scene. Travis Davis, the stepbrother to the star, has been arrested and held for questioning, although there is already rumor that he was being a 'vigilante,' coming to the rescue of his sister.

"Miss Davis was taken away in an ambulance to an undisclosed hospital, accompanied by a convoy of police cars. It seems she has not suffered any grave injuries. No word yet if the star is implicated in the deaths of these two men, who were believed to have been shot."

This soul-breaking news made my coffee go down the wrong way and I spluttered it over the lapel of my suit, transfixed as I was to the TV screen. It felt like a machine-gun was going off in my chest cavity my heart was racing so fast. The reporter's voice echoed in my head, even after the commercial break came on.

"Not suffered any grave injuries," the reporter had said. What the hell did that mean? Was she injured or *not*? Why was she being taken to the hospital? Did she pull the trigger? Fuck! My head was reeling, beads of sweat broke out on my brow.

Leo and a relative of his? Alexandre Chevalier had been right, then. Leo *was* involved in the kidnapping. But dead? *Dead?* The two men *shot?* I felt ridiculous standing here in Star's living room, with Leo's T-shirt in my pocket. *My* T-shirt that I'd lent him. So he *had* taken Star from me. I hung my head in remorse, shame, fear. But most of all, sadness.

And now my mind roved to another reality. Star would need a bloody good lawyer if they were implicating her in the shootings. My dad's attorney held no prisoners. He was a sharp, crooked bastard who you needed on your side. Thank God Star was still alive.

First, I needed to find out where they'd taken her. I stood up. "Janice, I'm off." My voice was a parched whisper. "Poor assistant's waiting for me in the car and I need to find Star—thanks for the coffee."

Janice nodded sadly, her arms around Fierce, finding solace in his canine empathy. My dog could always tell when people were unhappy and would respond with little licks, or nuzzling his nose against your neck.

"Keep Fierce for me today, would you?" I said, knowing that his dog walker would be by later to take him to Runyon Canyon, but that Janice needed him. "You can hang out together, if that's okay with you? I'll let you know the second I locate Star."

"Sure," she said. "Thanks. I just hope to God Star isn't in the hospital wing of some goddamn women's prison. I somehow feel responsible," she said. "If only I had forced my way into the lot that day, and she hadn't gotten in the car with Leo."

I laid my hand on her shoulder. "It's not your fault," I assured her. "But I know how you feel."

THE NEXT TIME I opened my eyes I saw a figure hovering over me. Not Leo this time. My body jerked instinctively but I felt woozier than ever, and when I went to shoo this person away, my arm was hindered by the entrapments of an IV punched into my vein.

"You just stay nice and calm, honey," a woman's voice soothed. She had a southern accent. "You've had a pretty rough day and it ain't even nine a.m!" She chuckled and leaned over me. "You've been crying out in your sleep, sugar. Tossing and turning, screaming out the name of 'Leo'—you was having some complicated nightmare."

"I was *dreaming*?" I focused on the person and saw that it wasn't a woman after all, but a man. With a very camp, gay voice that sounded female. He was dressed in a nurse's uniform.

"Dreaming like crazy," he clarified. "Whimpering and crying out."

"No! It wasn't a dream; it was real. I had a visitor. A man."

"Nobody has passed into this room, believe me. There are two policemen outside. You've caused quite a sensation, young lady. You're on the news non-stop. The sedatives I administered? They can sometimes cause pretty funky dreams. I'll give you something else, though, to take the edge off."

But I want the edge. If it means being with Leo— even if only in my dreams. "You say 'policemen?' Where am I?" My speech was slow as if I'd drunk a bottle of vodka. I thought of Leo and wished we'd had some shots together. Wished I'd let him take me last night. For real. I wished a lot of things concerning Leo.

"You're in the hospital, honey."

My eyelids threatened to close again but I

didn't want to sleep right now; I wanted to know what the hell was going on. But my thoughts were mixed and hazy—a cocktail of confusion.

"Are you *sure* I was dreaming? It was so real. Every tiny, miniscule detail."

"Yes, ma'am, you was just locked tight into a dream. Couldn't wake you up! You're stressed, honey, and that's not surprising. No wonder, after all you've been through. Lucky your brother came to your rescue, or you could have died."

"Travis?" I slurred. "My brother? He's saying he *saved* me?"

"That's right, apparently he saved your skinny ass from them Russian gangster kidnappers."

"No!" I protested, but my words were a whisper. My hands traveled down my body and I could no longer feel the straitjacket. Proof! Proof that Leo *was* here and Leo took it off of me! "I need to get up! I need to talk to the FBI!"

"They're comin' later to see you. They need a statement. You rest, now. You've been sedated— that's why you're so sleepy—because you need to get your strength back. You were quite a wildcat this morning! Scratchin' and screamin.' Hollerin' like a banshee. We had to strap you down so you didn't hurt yourself. Or anyone else."

"Leo undid those straps and freed me—he was *here*. I swear."

The male nurse giggled. "It was *me*, honey. I took that thing off. Who is this Leo? Isn't that the name of one of them kidnappers? Don't be afraid, baby—you're safe from them now." The male nurse exhaled a long sigh and continued chattily, "Who woudda thought I'd have Star *Davis* as my patient?" He chuckled again, his laugh catchy and tuneful. "Good Lord, this has been one *exciting* day! You know, I had to sign a confidentiality agreement? You can imagine my curiosity—and then it turned out to be you! Wait till I tell my niece—she be screamin' for your autograph. She just loved you in that sci-fi film, what was it called?" he said, slipping a needle into my vein.

"*Over The Moon*," I tried to reply, but what came out was more like *Ozemoo*.

"You shoudda won an Oscar for that part."

"I need to talk to—" but my words fell silent, my body numb—just like the old days when I was using—and I floated back into a deep, lonesome sleep, with no one in the world to hear me.

PRODUCTION
Shining Star

DIRECTOR
Jake Wild

DATE
June

SCENE
Driving around

TAKE
8

CAMERA
Jake Wild

"TURN THE RADIO up, will you, Biff?"
My car was new—a flashy, black, model S Tesla—electric—and with so many new-fangled gadgets, and with the controls on the steering wheel that I left it to Biff's expertise. Having had my drivers' license confiscated from me had been a pain in the arse, but now I'd grown accustomed to Biff chauffeuring me about, and I was beginning to prefer it to driving myself.

The voice sounded almost chatty, the way newscasters' voices often do. As if even the worst news somehow needs to be 'sold' to the highest bidder.

"Travis Davis, Star Davis's older stepbrother, came to her rescue in the early hours of the morning today, freeing her from the clutches of a pair of Russian gangster kidnappers, one of whom had infiltrated himself into the film she was working on—Skye's The Limit—with Hollywood director, Jake Wild. Nothing has been verified, and Mr. Davis is still being detained by police after having admitted to manslaughter in self-defense, and in defense of his stepsister with whom he is apparently very close. It seems that he had been following Star in an attempt to protect her. He told reporters that this was not the first time that she had been stalked, although this time the consequences were far more serious. More, later, on this extraordinary story. A plane has crashed over—"

Biff cut off the upbeat voice and changed stations—on came an old song from the 1970s, "I'm Not In Love" by 10cc. *Big boys don't cry.*

Like hell they don't.

This new persona that everyone had invented for Leo just didn't make sense to me. Had I been *that* blind to his charm and talent? He seemed like a true person: generous, kind and thoughtful, with such a fun, carefree sense of humor. I'd never known anyone like Leo before, and I'd considered him a true friend. Yeah, he was a bit of a party boy, but so what? He had a good heart (or so I'd thought). This news was beyond shocking, on every level.

I'd never heard Star talk about her stepbrother in a flattering light, yet he was suddenly this 'hero'—I didn't buy this whole story—something was off.

"Where are we going?" Biff asked.

"Just drive. I'm going to find out. Keep driving."

"My pleasure," she said, accelerating. "Being behind the wheel of this Tesla is better than multiple orgasms."

I smiled. The idea of butch Biff having orgasms seemed like an anomaly. I guessed she was the "man" in her relationship, if she had a girlfriend at all. I was tempted to ask but didn't want to get too personal. I pulled out my cellphone from my jacket. "I'm going to phone the LAPD—find out where Star is."

WHEN I AWOKE, the male nurse was gone. I was still woozy, the drugs coursing through my veins, reminding me of the state I was in for half of my teens. It felt like I was hanging out with an old loyal friend again, and the scary thing was? It felt great. Tears don't come when you're pumped full of drugs. You're numb. Things don't hurt you as much. Emotions simmer on the back burner, or bury themselves deep into your subconscious, ready for a rainy day, when you spill out all your ugly feelings to your shrink, or pour a Bloody Mary over a supermodel at an awards ceremony.

I sat up and looked around the stark white room. Nobody knew I was here because last time I was in the hospital, the room was bursting with color; you couldn't move for all the flowers and baskets of fruit, balloons, and teddy bears. I was ominously alone.

I thought back to what the nurse told me. That fucker Travis had spun them a web of bullshit; he'd "saved" me! Yeah, right. And he was obviously now pinning the kidnapping on Leo. Had I really been *dreaming*? I let my hand run down below my waist between my legs. I was moist there but not sore. Nothing seemed to have changed. Nobody had ravaged me. I was still a virgin. A virgin, who'd had an intensely realistic and erotic dream.

Words punched through my brain, pinching my heart:

Leo is dead.

Leo is dead.

Leo is dead.

I needed to know for sure; I wanted a straight answer from them. I ripped the IV out of my arm, swung my legs over the bed, and balancing myself, carefully planted my wobbly feet on the floor. I felt the welcome high rush to my head and thought of Mom. She was always stoned on prescription drugs. Where was Dad? Where was Mindy? Janice? Why was nobody here? Did *anyone* know where I was?

There was a jug of water by my bedside and I drank down two glasses without stopping to breathe. My stomach was concave. I hadn't eaten for several days now; probably why they'd given me a drip.

I stood up, using the bed to steady me, and shuffled my way to the bathroom to have a pee. I glanced in the mirror and saw a gaunt girl who looked like shit: sallow, with bags under her eyes, and stringy, greasy hair. I washed my hands and the crusted sleep out of my eyes, left the bathroom and padded in my bare feet—someone had removed my thigh-highs and bra—to the door.

When I opened it, two burly guys in uniform blocked my path. "Nurse!" one cried. "Call Detective Johnson. The suspect has woken up."

Suspect? What the hell is going on?

PRODUCTION
Shining Star

DIRECTOR
- Jake Wild

DATE
- June

SCENE
- Janice confesses

TAKE
10

CAMERA
- Jake Wild

B IFF AND I had been driving around in vain for ages. Nobody knew a thing. Not the Chevaliers, not the LAPD, where we had visited and come away with nothing. Hours had passed. The news flash earlier had made me nervous. I dialed a number I didn't think I'd ever need: the Inmate Information Line. I pressed each number slowly: 213 473-6100.

The line was still ringing. Finally someone picked up. I asked them if by any chance a Star Davis was being detained.

"Star Davis? the voice echoed. "No, nobody

has been arrested by that name."

"The movie star, surely you've heard of her?" I said, my voice a cleaver.

"I sure have, and I heard the news on the radio, but I do not have a Star Davis in my database."

Then I remembered; "Star" wasn't her real name. Had I even asked her what her real name was? Fuck! Still, the fact that she hadn't been arrested calmed me.

The whole day had gone by and I'd achieved nothing at all. Without knowing where Star was it was useless.

Biff and I were now in a parking lot, eating take-out food. I was just about to dial Chevalier's number for the umpteenth time, when the news flash cut through on the car radio again.

"More on Star Davis," the voice chirped.

"Turn it up, Biff." I bit into my taco but stopped chewing so I could hear every word.

"Secret sources, coming from inside the jail itself, have been leaked via Twitter newsfeed only moments ago, revealing some groundbreaking news. Travis Davis, the

stepbrother of Star Davis has now gone back on his previous statement earlier today. He no longer claims responsibility for shooting his sister's kidnapper, Leo Turgenev. It looks as if the Oscar-winning movie actress herself has just been accused by her brother of involuntary manslaughter of the kidnapper, the 26-year-old Ukrainian who had been working alongside her on *Skye's The Limit*, directed by Jake Wild.

"Mr. Turgenev and his uncle, 48-year-old Boris Turgenev, were holding the actress in a disused high-rise building in Downtown, Los Angeles.

"Star Davis's stepbrother, Travis Davis, discovered the actress in a state of, I quote, 'weakness and terror' after she had been nearly starved by the pair of criminals, who had issued a demand for payment from the producers of the movie studio, HookedUp Enterprises, who are making the film, *Skye's The Limit*, on which Miss Davis had been working up until her disappearance last Friday.

"Acting as a vigilante, Mr. Davis broke into the building in the early hours of this morning. He said a fight broke out between the two Ukrainian men—allegedly over money—and Boris Turgenev was strangled by his nephew, Leo. Mr. Davis is now claiming that his sister— who has played the roles of vigilantes in movies, and who *is no stranger to weapons—managed to get her hands on the gun and pull the trigger, instantly killing her other adversary, Leo Turgenev, with whom she had first disappeared last week.*

Forensic tests have apparently been taken out. Both the siblings' fingerprints are on the weapon that was used to kill Mr. Turgenev, and each tested positive regarding residue of gunfire on their clothing and respective bodies, so the tests are inconclusive—the truth still unknown. Mr. Davis has told police that his sister was, and still is, suffering from shock, memory loss, and Stockholm Syndrome concerning her kidnapper, Leo Turgenev. Star Davis has a history with drugs, alcohol, and violence— this is her third arrest."

It was as if I had no limbs; I felt pathetic, not being able to do anything. I knew that Star had the right to be let out on bail. But they also had the right to hold her for seventy-two hours until a court arraignment. She had the right to a phone call, maybe a couple. But Star hadn't called me. And then I remembered: as far as she was concerned, I was still with Cassie. To me it was as if a lifetime had passed—Cassie was well gone. But

Star didn't know that. Why would she be turning to me for help? She probably didn't want anything to do with me. I called Janice again, for the twentieth time that day, to find out if she knew anything and to check up on Fierce. She hadn't been picking up. This time she did. She was crying.

"I saw the news," she said between snivels.

"Un-fucking-believable," I said. And it was. I could hardly believe any of it. "Did Star call you by any chance?"

"Star didn't kill Leo," she said.

"No, I could never imagine she'd do a thing like that. I'm so confused Janice—I don't know what the fuck's going on; if Leo was involved or not. I keep going back and forth in my mind as to whether he was guilty or not. Can't get anything out of the LAPD and don't even know where the fuck Star is. Have you heard anything? I've been calling you all day."

"Yeah, Star used up one of her precious phone calls with me," Janice revealed.

I felt instantly jealous of their friendship, and reminded myself how I'd fucked things up.

"Her best friend, Mindy," Janice went on, "has

been the only person allowed to visit today. I think when someone's arrested they only get one visitor, even when they're Star Davis."

"I believe that's true. So what else can you tell me?"

"I'm scared," she wavered. "And I don't know what to do."

"Janice, with all due respect, this isn't about you, it's about what we can do for Star. What did she *say*?"

"She wants your lawyers and the Chevaliers' lawyers, and every top-shot lawyer in Hollywood to team up and prove Leo's innocence."

Stockholm Syndrome, they'd said. If Leo *had* kidnapped her along with his uncle, then they were right, although from what I'd read it usually took several weeks for that to happen. And if he hadn't kidnapped her—well—she'd obviously fallen in love with him. It wasn't as if they'd just met. We'd all been working together, and hanging out a lot. Leo and Star got along incredibly well, anyway. It was absurd to be feeling jealous of a dead man, but I couldn't help myself. "I can do that for her," I told Janice. "I can get a team of lawyers on it.

Where is she now?"

"In the medical wing of the LAPD Sheriff's Department, with drips and shit. She was severely dehydrated. In shock."

Well why the fuck hadn't someone told me that when I'd called or gone there? I'd heard about the medical services unit within the Los Angeles County Sheriff's Department, the second largest detention center in the country. In other words, she *was* in police custody. Under arrest.

Janice's voice hitched with another bout of tears. "Everybody's accusing everybody."

"You mean Star's stepbrother is blaming her for Leo's death?"

Janice was silent. She seemed more concerned with herself than with Star. "I don't know what to do," she repeated.

"Just be there for Star, Janice. Do what she asks of you, keep your phone handy in case she calls."

"I should have said something; but I didn't want to be disloyal, I . . ."

"Janice, if you have something to say, fucking say it."

She hung up on me. Shit, maybe I had been a bit harsh on her.

I CALLED CHEVALIER AGAIN, hoping he'd bloody well pick up this time. Pearl Chevalier was the producer, but for some reason her husband seemed to be involved in all her projects. "Involved" to say the least. He tended to commandeer her time. The jealous type, perhaps? Possessive? I now identified with that irritating flaw.

Since I'd met Star I'd never felt an overwhelming urge to own a woman before—the idea seemed old-fashioned and absurd. But there was something about Star that made me want, not only to look after her, but to "possess" her too. Not just sexually, but to *own* her feelings, or at least, be responsible for them in some way. Make her live through me. Was that narcissistic? Egotistical? Maybe. But I loved working with her, experiencing her, and I longed for her to feel the same. I embraced that team spirit, that creative drive, and when she succeeded, I did too, and vice versa. When she laughed, I felt her happiness buzz through me—literally, *through* me—and it brought me more pleasure than anything. And now I was terrified that she wouldn't be able to continue. To carry on filming *Skye's The Limit*. Which would mean I'd lose her completely.

Finally, Chevalier picked up. He'd seen the latest news on TV. I emphasized the importance of Star not giving a statement unless she had an attorney there—I hoped she had her wits about her.

"Star wants to prove Leo's innocence," I told him, "and wants a team of lawyers, yours, and mine, on the case. Personally, Leo's the least of our worries right now. He's dead; there's nothing we can do for him. It's Star's interest we care about, not bloody Leo's. You've heard of the OJ Simpson case, right?" I asked.

"Of courrrrse," Chevalier said, his accent more French than ever.

"I don't know about France, but here in the States, justice is all about having the best fucking lawyer money can buy."

"I have a great criminal lawyer named Neil Bernstein," he offered. "So what happens in this country?" he asked, "when someone's arrested in the State of California?"

"Well, if you've been arrested and charged with an offense, the police must bring you before a court as soon as is reasonably possible, if they can't take you to court immediately, which might be the case with Star as it seems she has a medical condition."

"Right now, who gets to decide whether to hold her in a cell, or wherever, until her first court appearance?"

"Right now? The police; if they decide she's low risk they'll release her on bail."

"And the exact terms of bail here?" he asked.

"Being on bail means you're released on conditions, including that you turn up at court when you're required to. You don't have a *right* to be given bail in these situations—it's up to the police to decide whether or not to release you. That's why she needs a bloody good lawyer. Now! I'm not sure who she usually uses, but judging by the last time she got arrested, he or she wasn't the brightest. So we need to get our attorneys down there ASAP," I said. "I'll call mine, too, and they can sort it out between them."

"Fine," he agreed. "Let them both go—she may need all the help she can get.

People like nothing more than to see a celebrity fall. And Star?" Chevalier said. "It looks like she's really in the *merde* this time."

THE SECOND I hung up, Janice called again. I rolled my eyes. I wondered how Star could have had such a self-centered person as her assistant all these years.

"What is it, Janice?"

"It's my fault. All of it."

"I don't have time for this, Janice, I need to call the lawyers, like *now*."

"Travis did it."

"I would say that's likely, but we don't know for sure."

"He kidnapped Star."

I froze with attention and listened while she told me a detailed story about how Travis had become friendly with Boris Turgenev and plotted with him to kidnap Star. How nobody was meant to get hurt, that it was all a mess and that Travis hadn't meant any harm, but that Leo hadn't been involved in any wrongdoing.

"And you're telling me this *now*, even though you knew all along?" I asked, relief that my friend Leo wasn't the bad guy after all.

"Yes," she whispered. "I'm so sorry."

"And how the fuck do you have all this information?"

"Because Travis," she answered, "is my half-brother."

"Whoa, go back. Travis is *Star's* stepbrother, right?"

"Yeah, but her dad isn't her biological father. He's mine and Travis's."

This was beginning to sound like a daytime soap. "Does Star know this intimate family history?"

"No."

"So why the secrecy?"

"My father never told me I was his. But he was a friend of the family, my family, and that's why I babysat for Star when she was young. He was having an affair with my mom. Then I found out, years later, *after* I became her assistant. It's complicated. And when I found out the truth? I bonded with Travis. But Star and Travis pretty much hated each other, and I didn't want to lose my job or her confidence in me, and it was uncomfortable being piggy in the middle, so I didn't say anything."

I wanted to punch the bitch, but I tried to remain calm, my voice even. "So all this time you knew about Travis's plan to kidnap Star?"

"No! Maybe. I mean, I *guessed*. I wasn't involved, but—"

"Save your sob story for a rainy day, Janice. The main thing is you get your arse down to the police station, *now*, and clear this shit up. Your brother Travis is lying! Star is being accused of involuntary *manslaughter*, for fuck's sake, and with her past and criminal record, a jury might just believe that sonnovabitch is telling the truth!"

"I know, that's why—"

"I'm coming to collect you right now and we'll go there together. Okay? And Janice?"

"Yeah?"

"Thanks for speaking up. Not everyone admits to being wrong."

11
Star

IF YOU ASKED me now to go into details about everything that ensued the next seventy-two hours, I couldn't. It was, and still is, a blur. Between all the police interrogation and attorney interviews I was in a total daze. I should have been looking out for myself, but I was cocooned in my new, buzzy, blanketed world of prescription tranquilizers and sleeping pills, and whatever else I could lay my hands on that the doctors were willing to hand out. Being a movie star does have its perks. Or not. Depending on your perspective.

I knew that I was being weak, letting myself be wooed back to my old ways. I *knew* that, but I was also aware that it was the only thing that would keep me going each day. I didn't want to let the pain of Leo's death take over. I was a coward, I chose the easy way out: by keeping my mind numb I could function just fine.

The prescription drugs buffeted me from the whiplash of knowing that Janice, the person I thought was my most trusted friend in the world, aside from Mindy, had betrayed me. She was the one who had alerted Travis. I had called her that day, to come and collect me from the lot after filming, but ended up going with Leo instead. She knew I was on my way home, where Travis was waiting with his big Dexter needle.

Did she know the details? Did she know he was going to kidnap us? I'll never be sure. Once someone has lied to you about their whole life, then there is no more deceit to scrape out of the barrel. Janice betrayed me. Leo was dead. Travis had tried to get me slung in jail for manslaughter, pin the kidnapping on Leo, not to mention the fact that he was the goddamn kidnapper *himself*, along with the sleazy uncle. To add insult to injury, when Jake had gone to my house, apparently Janice was using it as her own. Which would have been fine if she had been my true friend. I knew all along that Travis was a scumbag, but Janice broke my heart.

Luckily, because of Travis being such a dumbass and tracing my calls, the police had been surveying him. He denied stalking me, saying he wanted to protect me as he "suspected something was up." Even I don't know the details of how it was they tracked me to the high-rise in Downtown LA—I supposed that Travis had unwittingly led them there—but by this point I didn't even care anymore—didn't care if I was dead or alive.

I had nobody. My father . . . "father" was more interested in his real blood children than me. (P.S. another humdinger piece of news—Janice and Travis being related.) I had been his cash cow for all these years and now that Travis would be going to trial, and no doubt found guilty, and that Janice had "betrayed her own brother" as Dad put it, I was officially family-less.

I held a memorial for Leo, the one time I let my emotions get the better of me, but apart from that I kept my feelings buried deep down in my gut, saving them for moments in front of the camera. At least my misery would be useful.

The camera . . .

The only thing that had never let me down.

My only comfort was work. *Leo is dead. Leo is dead.* That was my mantra, and all I could think of.

"STAR, SWEETIE," Jake said, as he took me by the arm. I was back at work, several weeks later into filming. I had insisted upon going back to work the second I got released and found not guilty of any wrongdoing, thanks to the heavy team of lawyers that Jake and the Chevaliers had organized. I was still being watched by the studio—now more than ever, in fact. But most of our scenes were on location so there was no need to live with Jake anymore. I was either in my trailer, or a hotel, with a twenty-four seven bodyguard, until filming was over.

We were now on location in Wyoming. My character Skye was in a dingy motel, on the run. We had a scene in a gas station—a hold-up. It brought back memories:

Leo.

Blood.

Leo.

Love.

I popped another something-or-other-into my mouth, washing it down with mineral water.

I had a real shrink now, not that pussy therapist Narissa Deal who didn't want to give me a prescription. No. I had an old-school doctor who believed it was better to prescribe tranquilizers than have a suicide on his hands. He was fearful I could tip over the edge. So he pretty much gave me whatever I wanted to get me through each day.

Jake had been keeping a close eye on me too. He was suffering from guilt about the whole Leo thing. He'd lost a friend. I admitted to him how I felt about Leo; that although we'd been locked up for less than a week, terror and loneliness had bonded us. Sometimes Jake would end up spending the night, dozing off on the couch in my trailer. He was sleeping, eating and breathing *Skye's The Limit*. We both were. It was our way of coping.

It was our life. This movie had become like our surrogate child, drawing us so close to each other it was almost unhealthy. Our creation. Our baby.

But Jake was also sleeping and breathing *me*. Star/Skye—we were interchangeable. Why do so many actors end up falling in love with their co-stars or directors? And why is Hollywood one big broken marriage? It's easy to do the math. The sheer amount of creative time, the hours, and the intensity of the scenes, make it so. Jake was falling for me, little by little. He needed me—needed Skye. But I'd worked in this business for too many years to succumb. Directors were dangerous. A director "falling in love" with his leading lady was a way of extracting an amazing performance out of her. Such a Hollywood cliché. And in my state? Leo was the perfect excuse, or reason, to keep Jake at arm's length.

Jake held onto my arm, bringing me back from my thoughts, his voice coaxing, his touch careful, but deliberate. "Star. I need more emotion in this scene. I need your anger. Skye's at a moment in the movie that she really hates men." Then Jake whispered in my ear, "You're having pizza with

Travis and Boris and your dad. I want to see it in your eyes."

My dad . . . yeah, he'd hurt me more than I imagined possible. Travis had always been a lost cause, and Boris, he was easy to hate because of what he'd done to Leo. I could feel burning behind my eyes, smell the anger on my own breath, mingling with the vodka on Jake's breath.

Vodka: the sneaky drinker's drink. *Think I can't smell it, Jake? It takes one to know one, buddy.*

EVER SINCE I'd told Jake that I was in love with Leo, he had started drinking. An excuse to revert to his addictive ways? Or maybe to keep me company . . . two fuck-ups making a movie together. The beauty was, though, nobody knew we were numbing our brains. We were professionals. We could smile and perk up at the snap of a finger. We had them all fooled.

Except Biff, who was onto us. She rushed around picking up our pieces, all day long. Making sure we drank enough mineral water. Putting me to bed. Waking me. Bringing me food. Buying my tampons, even knowing when my period was. She read books to me to help me sleep, brushed my hair, polished Jake's shoes. Brought him tea. Brought me coffee. Fed me dark chocolate that I washed down with Chateauneuf du Pape, a new favorite of mine, and when Jake wasn't glugging down a sly gulp of heavy booze, he'd join me.

Jake and I were maudlin, introvert, extrovert, talked about philosophy, and acting, and camera angles, and Orson Welles, and *Black Orpheus*, and how Al should have won the Oscar for *The Godfather*, and why we loved Audrey more than Katharine. Jake and I—I realized—had slowly and unwittingly merged into best friends. We'd hold hands. We became—little by little—inseparable.

I stared into space a lot of the time, wondering what my purpose in life was, wondering why I was alive and Leo was dead.

Meanwhile, Jake was revealing his feelings for me: bouquets of hand-picked wildflowers, little gifts, handmade cards, or simply regarding me with narrowed eyes for minutes on end.

Isn't that typically the way? Men: they always arrive late—too late—to the party.

"Marry me, Star," he said one evening, his voice a slur—he'd been drinking, as usual—I was going to take that "proposal" with a grain of salt. We were lying on the roof of his car, looking up at the stars, trying to find the Big Dipper.

I laughed. "You're just saying that," I said. "The minute filming's over, you'll forget all about me."

"No I'm not just saying it, actually. And I'll never forget you. I happen to love you."

Happen to. He was full of shit. "I love you too, Jake. As a friend."

"But you love Leo more." Jake sounded like a little boy at kindergarten. That's the kind of thing a child would say. Boy, was he fucked up.

"He's dead," I pointed out.

"Right."

"Loved, not love," I said.

"But you're still in love with him. In love with a ghost."

I squeezed Jake's hand. "Yeah, you're right, I'm in love with a ghost." *Keep him at arm's length,* my voice told me. *Jake is dangerous. He breaks women's hearts. He's a bad boy, even if he'd like to be good.*

"You need to get over it," he ordered in a gruff voice. "You can't hold on forever."

"He broke my virginity, Jake" I countered, believing my half-lie, half-truth.

What I said took Jake's breath away. Wounded his pride. I knew I'd broken his heart, as far as he had a heart. And I was aware that he only wanted me because I told him I was in love with someone else. But Jake had had his chance with me and blew it. Still, I could hear his hurt. Literally. I put my hand on his heart and felt his boyish pangs. But I didn't say anything to un-do it.

Mainly because I was too numb to feel.

IT WAS THE beginning of December. My mind wandered to six months earlier, to the month of June, when Jake and I had started filming *Skye's The Limit*. Sometimes, it felt like yesterday and other days, a lifetime. I thought about Jake a lot because I was in London right now, meeting with producers about doing a Harold Pinter play at the Almeida Theatre. Jake was a Londoner, originally. *Skye's The Limit* was all wrapped up and now in post-production. I was being offered two or three film projects a day by various studios, but was turning everything down because nothing grabbed me.

Why was I toying with the fantasy of doing theatre? To prove myself, maybe? But my head was telling me 'no.' I was in no fit state to act on stage every night. Who was I kidding? I was a movie star, who got to do re-takes if I fucked up my lines. Theatre was no joke. So when the phone rang at my hotel, where I was now, for some reason I wasn't surprised when I heard a familiar voice at the other end of the line.

"I'll be at your hotel in an hour," Jake said, without even saying hi. "And I'll show you my home town."

I wanted to say, *Speak of the Devil,* but I replied, "The Crown Jewels? Big Ben?"

"No, that shit's for tourists. We'll just hang out

and you can get a feel for the real London."

I was staying at a boutique hotel called Hotel 41, choosing it because of its penthouse Conservatory Suite which had a glass ceiling, so that when you lay in bed you could look up at the city stars. It also had a quaint Victorian fireplace with a blazing fire. The perfect place to hide out in a dream-drug-induced state. I decided that theatre was out of the question until I cleaned up my act—whenever that would be.

"Come on over," I said. "Take me out for a night on the tiles." I knew I'd hurt Jake, but I was also aware that it was more a blow to his ego, rather than real pain. What did Jake know about pain? He wasn't in love with me. It was lust. It was about his pride and desire for conquest. It was an obsession he had with me, nothing more. He didn't know the meaning of the word love.

Let him come over, I decided. I'd give him whatever he wanted. I didn't even care anymore.

PRODUCTION
Shining Star

DIRECTOR
Jake Wild

DATE
Winter

SCENE
The deflowering

TAKE
12

CAMERA
Jake Wild

I HADN'T EXPECTED Star to accept my invitation, and I panicked. *Where the fuck should I take her that wouldn't cause a media sensation?* Her voice on the telephone sounded drowsy, and I knew what that meant. She was still using. That made two of us. I'd been on a sex and drinking binge since we'd finished filming. The only good thing I could say about it was that I had managed to be careful every time: I was meticulous about using condoms. Other than that, I had given in to every temptation, every piece of sexy arse that came my way. But all I could think of, every time I plunged my cock into some random pussy: some top model, or actress, or TV celebrity—was how I wished it were Star.

She'd broken my fucking heart.

I was second-hand goods, which hurt like hell. And after all this time away from her since the film had wrapped, anger was building inside me. I thought about fucking her a lot; fucking the *nonsense* out of her. Fucking the obsession she had about a phantom out of her, for good. I was desperate for her to lay Leo to rest.

When I entered the lobby of her hotel, my heart started palpitating with nerves. I sauntered to the bar and ordered a stiff double whiskey to calm myself.

For some reason drink has never hurt my libido, and with all the fantasies of late about fucking some sense into Star, when she opened the door to her penthouse suite, wearing nothing but a skimpy silky robe, I got an instant hard-on.

"You're early," she said, hovering at the door without letting me in. "I've just got out of the tub. I'll put on some clothes and then you can take me on a night-time sight-seeing tour."

"This is all the sight-seeing I need," I said, my eyes roving over her body. The curves of her perky tits were barely covered by the thin fabric. "Invite me in," I demanded.

Her lips quirked up into her signature crooked smile. "What are you, a vampire?"

"Something like that."

"Well come on in then, I have a thing for vampires."

She was high as a fucking kite. A nice man would have been a gentleman and not taken advantage, but I wasn't a nice man; I was bad. Through and through.

I stepped up to her, my whiskey lips on hers. "Get on the bed," I breathed into her mouth. I need to fuck you."

"Sure, why not."

"*Really?*"

"Feel free," she said, her half-mast eyes allowing themselves to trail down to the bulge in my trousers. "We might as well get it over with. Once you've had me you'll leave me alone, so let's just fuck, Jake. Get me out of your system."

Her words were painful. So painful that the

only thing that could numb my feelings was sex.

I ripped off her robe, my hands sliding all over her body, my tongue on her neck, her shoulders, her tits, her mouth, sucking like the vampire I was—biting and nipping. I pushed her roughly onto the bed. Her eyes were lazily dazed and she was calm as hell, not resisting me in any way. My cock was fucking massive, and I wasn't in the mood for foreplay. I wanted her now—yesterday. I'd wanted her my whole life. I unbuckled my belt and unbuttoned my trousers, letting my cock spring free.

"All I think about every minute of every day, Star. Is you." I pushed her legs apart, spreading her wide. "I'm going to fuck you really hard, okay?" I tore off my linen shirt.

"You might as well," she drawled. "Then you can get me out of your system."

"That's right," I agreed. "I want to get this obsession out of my system." My hands were splaying her soft thighs wide, wide open. I observed her pussy, hot and wet like a ripe fruit, and I buried my face there, breathing her in, trying to calm myself down.

But it made my dick even thicker, even harder, the veins straining against my swollen size. I lashed my tongue all over her, sucking in her tasty juices, then with one hand under her arse, and with my other hand—my thumb inserted deep inside her cunt—I hauled her into the middle of the mattress, groaning as I did so. I popped my thumb into my mouth and sucked in her sweet taste. "Fuck, you're hot," I said. Her beautiful blond hair cascaded over her elegant shoulders, her lips were swollen where I'd bitten her on the mouth.

She lay languidly on the bed. Arching her back. "Come on, then, big boy, show me what you got."

"I've got a huge, great, big, horny cock that wants to fuck you senseless."

She laughed. "I'm already senseless, so come on, Jake, let's get this party going."

I blanketed her slim body with all of me, and thrust myself into her in one hard stroke—she cried out.

"You like that?" I said. "As much as you liked it with Leo?"

She didn't respond, and her silence tore through me. I pulled back, then drove myself in again. She was tight as fuck, the tightest I'd ever experienced, her walls squeezing and clenching me so keenly that I knew that this pussy would be my downfall. Forever. How wrong Star was. This wasn't getting her out of my system, but making it a thousand times worse. I needed this woman. And I needed this hot, tight, juicy cunt.

"I feel like a rag doll," she whispered, "that you're just using. Tell me you love me, Jake."

"Oh fuck yeah I love you," I growled, ramming back into her. "You're my every thought, my every fantasy. Forever, Star." I pulled back, but instantly missed the closeness, so plunged into her hard again, back and forth, punctuating my thrusts with words as I fucked her. "I. Love. You. Oh fuck, Star. Ob—" I pulled out slowly—"sessed. I'm. Ob" – I drove into her even deeper—"Sessed. Oh fuck, baby, I can't live without you."

I lifted her hips higher so her arse was even closer to me and could bury myself in really deep. And that's when she started to respond, raising her pelvis to meet mine, her calves wrapped tightly around my thighs, rubbing her clit against me every time I came down on her. Her nipples were peaked—I could feel them on my chest as my body slapped against hers. I growled in her mouth, my tongue inside, in a frenzy of carnal, stupefied love-lust, jealousy about Leo consuming every cell in my body.

Her legs started to stiffen and her hands clawed my arse, like a playful cat. "I'm coming, Jake . . . I'm coming."

I instantly exploded inside her. No condom for Star; I wanted to feel every bit of her. If she got pregnant? Good. *Then she'd be mine,* I thought, selfish in my inebriated haze.

I slowly, slowly pulled out. But I was still hard as fuck. I wanted more. *All* of her. I turned her over so she was on her stomach. She was floppy, relaxed. I stroked her softly up and down her crack. I wanted this perky little arse. Now. I wanted to claim every single inch of Star Davis's delicious body. I kneeled over her—droplets of my cum landing where she needed it. I massaged her there with my finger, lubricating her tight little orifice. My cock flexed at the thought of entering her. She groaned, evidently enjoying my attention; my fingers playing with her sensitive rosebud hole.

I slid my finger inside, little by little, and explored her, easing it in and out slowly, delicately.

Mine. All mine. Leo wouldn't have gone there, because he once told me he wasn't into anal sex. At least I'd be Star's first in this respect.

"What are you doing?" she whimpered. "It feels illicit."

"It is." I brought my other hand underneath her soaked pussy, cupping my palm over her mound, exerting a little pressure—but not too much—on her clit. I slid my thumb a tiny bit into her hot little behind and she gasped and moaned, wiggling beneath me. I needed her taste again. So I brought my wet hand from her juicy cunt to my mouth. But as I drew it to my lips, my fingers were covered with blood.

"You should have told me you had your period," I said. "Not that it matters to me, but for your sake." I looked at my dick. It too was bloody.

"I don't have my period," she murmured.

"There's blood everywhere, baby."

"Yeah, well, when you deflower a virgin, I guess that's what usually happens."

"Stop joking around, Star." I rolled her over so

she was lying on her back, facing me. "Look at me," I said.

She fluttered opened her lazy eyes and murmured, "Was I what you expected? Or are you disappointed?"

"You're playing head games with me, aren't you—saying you're a virgin?"

She looked up at the glass roof to the London stars. The last time we were lying on our backs together she was looking at stars.

"Well I'm not a virgin anymore," she sang in a child's voice.

What the fuck game was she playing? But it was true; when I'd eaten her pussy earlier, there hadn't been any blood. I would have tasted it, but she was sweet. "But what about Leo? You told me—"

"Sex with Leo was in my dreams. *After* he died. When we were locked up, he never went further than a kiss."

I looked at my bloodied hand. "You were a *virgin*? Tonight? Before I laid my hands on you? Before I *fucked* you?"

She didn't answer, just smirked as if the joke was on me.

"You were a *virgin?*" I echoed.

"Not anymore," she chanted.

I'd been such a jerk. "But I ravaged you! It must have fucking hurt."

"When you take a handful of Valium, nothing hurts."

I felt a lump in my throat. "It wasn't meant to be like *this*, Star. Why didn't you *say* something? I never would have—"

"You know what, Jake? Maybe you should just leave. I feel kind of dirty, like I've betrayed Leo. He was so sweet, so kind, so respectful. He never would have done what you did tonight. You know why? Because he genuinely *loved* me."

If I felt bad before, it was nothing compared to this. But she was right. I'd been a total prick; I deserved her rejection. "I'm so sorry, Star,"—I laid my hand on her shoulder—"please forgive me. I've behaved—"

She flinched, not letting me finish my sentence, "You've behaved the way you always do. Your dick controlling you. With no compassion, no thought for anyone, but yourself. I hope you got what you wanted, Jake. Hope you've got me out of your system now."

"Stop with the fucking 'out of your system' shit, Star! *You are my system*, don't you get that? Can't you *see* that?" Tears were welling in my eyes. This woman knew how to hit below the belt. And no, that's not a play on words. "I'm sorry," I said, my voice quiet. "I've fucked up royally this time."

She maneuvered herself away from me, crawled under the sheets, and then closed her eyes. "Night, Jake. Remember to take your iPhone with you when you leave. I don't want to be disturbed by your pretty girlies calling all hours of the night."

I sat up, too stunned for words.

"Off you go now." And then she rolled over and slipped into a deep, deep slumber.

FOR THE NEXT few weeks, Star ignored my calls. I couldn't blame her. After a while, I gave up. She didn't give a fuck about me. Thought I was a sleezeball, which I pretty much was. Even if she hadn't been a virgin, that was no way to treat a woman. I was a prize arsehole and my attitude had to change. I'd been using her love for Leo as an excuse to be a shit, to treat women badly. Sex with the others had become monotonous anyway—I wasn't even enjoying it anymore.

I was a sick fuck who needed help. No wonder she'd fallen for Leo. Women might fantasize about fucking and taming a man like me, but in the long run? That's just a fantasy. No decent female wants a womanizer to be her partner. I was on a train to fucking nowhere.

Daily, I busied myself in the editing room, and dealt with all the postproduction for *Skye's The Limit*. Star was lucky. She was done with the movie. She could put her mind to other things. Me? Seeing her face blown up on the screen every day when I went to work—larger than life—only did one thing: cement my love for her all the more.

The interesting thing was that our "liason" in London had done something to me. I genuinely no longer felt compelled to fuck around. The only thing I now wanted:

Was to make *love to Star*. And Star only.

But I feared it was too late. I'd blown any chances I might have once had.

13.
Star

PEARL CHEVALIER was impressive; the kind of woman I wanted to be when I grew up. She wasn't an addict, a screwed-up head-case like me. I thought that if I studied her long enough, perhaps I could be more like her.

We had arranged to meet at the airport in Burbank, and I expected to be flying with her on the Chevalier's private HookedUp jet, not be flown *by* her.

"Star," she said, as I stepped out of my limo. "How lovely to see you *not* in your prison uniform. You look great." She kissed me on the cheek and hooked her arm through mine. She was dressed in a very chic, pinstripe pantsuit, her blond hair swept up into an elegant chignon. She wore pearl stud earrings.

She was being polite. I didn't look great, or if I did, it was clever makeup. I'd learned a few tricks of the trade over the years and knew how to hide a multitude of sins: lifeless, sallow skin, and bags under my eyes from "lack of sleep." She gazed at me hard for a second, and I wondered if she could secretly tell that Ativan, Valium, and even the painkiller, Vicodin, were my new go-to buddies. I doubted it; she seemed like the sort of person who had never been a prisoner to her addictions like me.

"You're not scared of flying in small planes, are you?" she asked.

"Well, it depends who the pilot is," I said, trying to be smiley and normal.

"Me, I'm your pilot."

I grinned. One of those "say-cheese" Hollywood grins you do for photographers when your eyes don't crinkle, when only your mouth moves and your pearly-whites shine. I actually thought she was kidding. I'd seen her on set several times, but I was always too concentrated on work to pay much attention to her and her ironic sense of humor. The only time we'd had a deep conversation was when I initially talked her into giving me the role of Skye—but we had never hung out. So being invited to the Chevalier's for Christmas as their guest was a pretty big deal. And when we mounted the steps to the plane, and Pearl ushered me into the cockpit to take a look, and I realized she was serious about being the pilot, I nearly passed out. I could feel a drug-induced sweat breaking out on my forehead, and felt in my purse to make sure my little friends were there. They were, and the panic instantly subsided. In ten minutes I'd be able to go to the bathroom and pop whatever I needed.

Pearl settled into the pilot's seat and started fiddling with an array of fancy controls.

"*You're* flying this thing?" I asked, double-checking.

"Sure, why not? Learning to fly was a gift to myself. You know, I once nearly died from a silly fall at home—ended up in a life-threatening coma—and since then I vowed to do anything and everything in life that people consider 'risky'."

My eyebrows gathered together.

She laughed. "Don't be scared, Star, really. My co-pilot will be by my side—he's arriving any second."

"Alexandre?" I asked.

"No, my husband isn't interested in flying; he thinks I'm being very extravagant having my own plane. He's into cars. He says he likes to feel the road beneath him, makes him feel more grounded."

She was in her forties but looked so much younger, not just physically, but because of her *joie de vivre*. It was interesting that her husband, who was fifteen years her junior, didn't appear younger than her at all. They were the perfect match; one of those couples everybody wants to be. Beautiful, powerful, and most importantly: in love.

She winked one of her large blue eyes at me and tucked a stray lock of honey-blonde hair behind her ear. "Don't be nervous, Star." Her mouth lifted into a quirky grin. "I have some crazy memories of this little airport, you know."

"Being whisked off to glamorous resorts in

private jets?"

"No, nothing glamorous. It was before my husband and I tied the knot. I was a bit of an escape artist, to say the least."

"Well, men do like a chase," I said, thinking of Jake and all his girlies, and how good he must be feeling to have finally got me in the sack.

"Poor Alexandre, it's a wonder he put up with me." She looked at my luggage, which was nothing more than an overnight bag. "That's it? All you're bringing?"

"As you know it was a last minute decision to come along."

"Even better, now we have the perfect excuse to go shopping."

I SPENT A WEEK at the Chevalier's thousand-acre ranch in New Mexico, recuperating from life in general. It was set at the foot of a stunning mountain range; a secluded, secret place where they kept horses, went hiking and kayaking—a place, Alexandre told me—to escape the pressures of everyday life.

It was just what I needed. To get away from Hollywood and feel protected with my new adoptive family. It was warming to spend time with them—it *warmed* my soul. Alexandre couldn't take his eyes off Pearl; he laughed at things she said, and spending time with this couple and their three adorable children, gave me hope. One day. Maybe. If I could just shake the demons—both physical and metaphysical—out of my system.

One morning, Pearl and I were hanging out together by the indoor pool, just us. She'd been doing vigorous lengths, and I understood how she maintained her incredible figure. The kids, Louis, Madeleine, and little Lily, were with their dad out on a hike. He was an incredible father, often joking that he was a "househusband" and a "kept man" and that Pearl was the breadwinner. But his immense wealth—*their* wealth—was never ostentatious, and work didn't seem to take a priority in their marriage. In fact, their life was such a sickening fairy tale that at times it made me want to check myself into rehab, flush the shit out of my system and be perfect like her, so that I could meet a normal man like Alexandre Chevalier.

"I wish I could find happiness the way you have," I moaned, flicking listlessly through Vogue. I hadn't been swimming—didn't have the energy, and I could have drowned with all my nice prescription drugs flowing through my veins. I didn't have the motor skills to even do breaststroke. All I'd been doing was sleeping, because it was the only way I could hang out with Leo—in my dreams.

"Star, I'm old enough to be your mom."

"So?"

"So, you think my life was all sorted out at— how old are you now?"

"Twenty."

"Exactly! You're a baby, honey. I mean, you're not a *baby*, . . . you've seen and done more than most people have in a lifetime, and you're sophisticated, but in terms of the sheer number of years you've been breathing, you're only just starting out."

"I don't know," I said. "My life has been pretty fucked up. You're so *together*."

She laughed. "If you could have heard my internal monologues when I was in my twenties and thirties, and even at the time I met Alexandre, when I had just turned forty, you would have committed me to an asylum."

My mouth fell open. Perfect Pearl Chevalier? "You? Seriously? But you're a producer, a mom, a wife . . . so beautiful—"

"I was an insecure basket-case, Star. I won't go into detail now, but I had a few things happen in my past that knocked my confidence sideways."

I shook my head. "Well, I can't believe that you were *ever* unstable."

"Well, that's adorable of you, but my point is, you cannot expect at your age to have all the answers, and to not be affected by the kidnapping, Leo's death, and everything that ensued. You went through Hell. It was a *major* trauma—something that will haunt you for life. And it's okay to make mistakes and it's *okay* to run—you're still finding your feet."

"Run? I wish I had the energy," I quipped.

But Pearl carried on, "I totally understand. I ran from Alexandre because I was so fearful that I wasn't good enough for him, and that I'd lose him. So I ran before I had a chance to fail."

"But I'm not running!"

"Jake," she answered simply. One syllable: *Jake.*

"What's Jake got to do with this? It was Leo all along."

"Leo was your escape route. Leo, rest in peace, was gorgeous and sexy and kind and fun, et cetera et cetera, but he wasn't your soul mate, your *media naranja.*"

I laughed. "Half an orange?"

"It's a Spanish expression that pretty much means soul mate. When you cut an orange in two, if you put the two halves back together again, they make one perfect whole."

"But they're still two halves."

"Exactly. Two halves making one. You and Jake? You two hold something very, very special; don't give up. Even if you decide to take a break from each other—as would be wise right now— remember . . . you have a bond. I saw the way he used to look at you on set." Pearl raised her eyebrows knowingly. "Jake might just be your *media naranja.*"

"What? like two dysfunctional Hollywood casualty halves making up one, big whole fruitcake?" I laughed raucously, imagining us together and remembering our disastrous *rendezvous* in my London hotel, when he was drunk and I was high. "We're too screwed up for each other, Pearl."

"You think I'm 'normal'? Or Alexandre? You're *not* nutty as fruitcakes, you're just 'artists.'"

"Drama queen artists who'd probably destroy each other," I said.

"What you did together with *Skye's The Limit* is a work of art, Star. And you have so much in common. You were both raised in the movie industry. Look, things will sort themselves out in their own time, but all I can tell you is, *that man* is in love with you and he has a good heart, a good soul, despite his antics."

"He only wants me because he can't have me."

"He wants you because you're one of a kind. But Star?" she said, the 'Star' like a warning. "You *really* need to get your act together. For good this time."

"What do you mean?" I said, sounding shocked and innocent.

"You need to get straight. Those doctors that hand out pills like candy? They prey on sensitive people like you. But it's your decision, your choice. *You* are the only one who can help yourself."

"Pearl, you have it all wrong! Honestly. I just haven't been sleeping well, that's why I look tired. But I swear," I lied, my expression giving nothing away, "I haven't had a pill for two months. I'm clean as a whistle."

But she wasn't buying my bullshit. "When you're ready," she said, ignoring my denial. "You let me know. And I promise, I will help you."

CHRISTMAS WAS LIKE watching a feel-good commercial from the 1950's. Their house, which was haute-adobe (as in haute-couture) sparkled with decorations, and their children, the twins, Louis and Madeleine, were polite and funny and sparkled with candy-kissed adorability (is there such a word?) And little Lily, the youngest, with her white curls and cherubic face, sat on my knee and played with my hair and sang me nursery rhymes, and she too sparkled with cuteness, and Alexandre sparkled with the most-charming-Frenchman-alive-eat-your-heart-out-tall-dark-and-handsome-God's-gift-to-women, and Pearl sparkled because that's just who she is.

And there was I, high and lonely, the token fuck-up.

Not sparkling at all.

That was when I decided I had to definitively do something about my sorry-Star ass.

PRODUCTION
Shining Star

DIRECTOR
Jake Wild

DATE
March

SCENE
Star's trailer

TAKE
14

CAMERA
Jake Wild

I
T HAD BEEN months since I'd seen Star and I was nervous as hell. The last time we'd been together both of us were at our worst—she, high as a kite and inebriated—and me, well, I was plastered. But the worst thing of all was that I'd broken her precious virginity in a sleazy way, like the fuck-up I was. We had both relapsed and shown each other our dark, weak sides. Of course I still felt ashamed and sheepish, but we needed to clear the air. I needed her forgiveness. I wanted to be friends again, mainly because I missed her so much, and at this point I'd take any crumbs that

were offered; even stale ones.

Despite my having a GPS, her house—or rather, her land—was hard to find. People think of Malibu as being typically by the ocean, where movie stars live, which it is. But Malibu is also a large county next to LA, and parts of it so wild and remote, you'd swear you were in another country. India perhaps. There are raccoons, coyotes, gray foxes, badgers, and mountain lions, which live in the rough backcountry. I remembered coming here as a boy with my uncle to bird-watch and saw Cooper's hawks and golden eagles. And it was in this area that Star—one of the richest movie stars in the world—was now living.

In a bloody trailer.

Not only that, but the Santa Ana winds are famous for whipping up a lethal wildfire within seconds of starting. Her new abode was precarious, to say the least—not to mention earthquakes. She was remote, isolated; I couldn't see another house around for miles.

It was great to have the freedom of driving again. Not that I minded being chauffeured around by Biff, but I needed my privacy, and today was definitely one of those days. Star had called me out of the blue. She'd changed her cellphone number and nobody except her best friend Mindy, she told me, knew where she now lived. I felt privileged that she trusted me enough to let me in on her secret.

In the distance, I saw a rider on a horse, as my car bumped along the potholed "road". The rider came galloping towards me, fearless, like a character in a spaghetti Western, totally at ease with the horse as if they were one being.

It was Star.

I slowed my car to a few miles an hour and buzzed down the window. The horse whinnied and cut up the dusty ground with its hoof. It was a beautiful black stallion, its withers shiny from the exercise, its nostrils flaring with what seemed like self-assured arrogance. Star stroked his forelock.

"Good boy, Max. Good boy."

Seeing her caused my heart to jolt. When she beamed at me it was as if she smiled for nobody else in the world like that—only me. I smiled back, wishing my fantasy were true. People don't get to be movie stars just because. They have the *je ne sais quoi*, a devilish charisma, the uncanny ability to make you believe you're their best friend, and that you've known them all your life. I did know Star, but only a fraction of her, and I wished—so wished—that one day, we could become real friends again, the way we had been while filming. Discussing nonsense into the night. Best ever performances, best lighting, worst fuck-ups, where you got the best pizza in the world (I said Italy, she said New York), . . . I didn't dare wish for more than a smattering of our old friendship. That in itself was greedy, after what I'd done.

We didn't even say hello to each other, just locked eyes. It was as if she were trying to read my thoughts.

She just said, "Follow us. Don't overtake Max, though—he's competitive." She went straight into a canter, the horse's hind legs showing their power as they then lunged into a heavy gallop.

I laughed and put the car into gear, following the animal and the trail of dust, and the strange, unpredictable actress who had stolen my heart.

After a good fifteen minutes of trail, we came across a small wood of oak trees and there, in the dappled shade, was her humble trailer. She dismounted Max, swinging her leg high in one perfect arc, and jumped down as if she'd been riding all her life, then led him by the bridle to a tub of water, under the trees. By the trailer was a faded old pick-up truck, dented and dusty. Not in a million years would you have imagined that Star Davis, the spoiled, rich, Cristal-drinking brat that I had originally taken her for, lived here.

"It doesn't look like much, but I have cold sodas and some killer guacamole I made, and some chips and salsa that will blow your mind."

You blow my mind, I wanted to say, but I just grinned like a fool.

"Come in." She looked genuinely happy. Carefree. Not stoned. Not high. Her eyes were clear. She was a different person than the fuck-up I'd mercilessly taken advantage of that night in London.

"Star," I began. "I—"

"I know, you're sorry, you don't need to say it."

She stole the words out of my mouth. I realized . . . that's what Star did best: steal emotions, words, thoughts. That was her job.

"No, I wasn't going to say that," I lied. "I just wanted to tell you how great it is to see you."

"Oh, so you're *not* sorry?" She glared at me,

and for a second she had me fooled, 'til I understood she was joking. She smiled again and took me by the arm.

"This is the trailer you had during *Skye's The Limit*?" I said, for something to say. I felt pretty dumbstruck.

"Yup. I wanted to buy it from the studio, but the Chevaliers gave it to me as a gift. Don't be shy, come on in, Jake. Take a seat."

I awkwardly sat down, not taking my eyes from her. She looked different. Despite her torn jeans and cowboy gear, she looked sophisticated. Like a real woman, not a girl. She handed me an old-fashioned Coca-Cola bottle, ice-cold, with a stripy straw floating on top.

"To old times," she said, and we clinked bottles. "Not that I remember these bottles, you know, but I like the vintage feel. People wonder why I don't have a cool 1950's Airstream trailer instead of this, but I like the tacky trashy-ness of it, you know? It reminds me who I am."

I'd heard Star's "trailer-park-trash" nonsense before, and I wasn't buying it.

"You're beautiful, Star." The words came out before I could stop them. I hadn't come here to woo her, or try and convince her that I was the man for her. I knew that was futile.

"That's what Leo used to say to me."

A knife in my gut, in my heart. Why had I come here? What a fool!

But seeing the hurt that must have obviously been etched into my face she quickly said, "Well, 'used to'. . . that's silly to say when we hardly knew each other. I mean, what was it? I mean 'full-on' time. A few days?"

This was a one-eighty. Before, she had made out that Leo had been the love of her life. I chose my words carefully, not wanting to fall into that trap again. "A few days can seem a lifetime, Star, don't underestimate how mercurial time can be."

" 'How mercurial time can be' . . . great line, I like that. Did you know that Marlon Brando came up with some of his greatest lines, himself? 'I watched a snail crawl along the edge of a straight razor' in *Apocalypse Now* . . . that was *him*, he wrote that line into the movie."

"Not surprised, he was a genius," I said, wondering where this conversation was leading.

"You know, Jake, my whole life has been cinematic. I see everything in terms of a film.

Every line, every movement, every thought. And it's high time that changed."

"Like, how?"

"Like time I got out."

"You can't!" I shouted—the shout a mistake, my voice rumbling with dread. *What if I never work with my favorite actress again? What if our collaboration was a one-off?* The movie industry needed Star—we needed this shining star!

"Don't be selfish," she said. "I don't belong to anyone. I need to discover the real world. See the world through the eyes of a normal person. I need this, Jake. For me."

"Is that what this is all about? The trailer?"

"No. This is a simple solution—just for the time being—to escape the paparazzi."

"But Star, you're alone out here."

"I'm not alone. Mindy comes to see me every day."

"After all that happened? You're here without a bodyguard—it's crazy!"

"I carry firearms."

I shook my head. "Bad idea. Someone could take the gun from you and use it against you. You see all the accidents that happen on the news!

Guns are dangerous, Star."

"It would be dangerous if I hadn't done all that kick-ass training for *Pedigree Angel*—I know how to fire a gun, can kick-box too."

"You *took* that part of the corrupt female cop?"

"I did. But then I changed my mind. Angie's doing it now."

"Angelina?"

She nodded, took a long sip of her Coke, then looked me hard in the eye. "I'm going away, Jake. And I wanted you to know."

My pulse started racing. "Where?"

"Not even I know yet. I'm going backpacking around the world. With Mindy."

"Two women alone, backpacking, you don't even know where? That's a mad idea. Everyone will recognize you for starters."

"Tomorrow I'm cutting off all my hair and dying it black. People know me by the name of Star. They have no idea who Diane Davis is, which is on my passport. I know from experience—when I've done movies—people expect you to be who you are, not what you can become. When Bobby de Niro was cruising around New York working as a taxi driver for real before he started filming, nobody said, 'Hey, I took a cab ride today and guess who was my driver?' You don't get recognized in places people don't expect to see you."

"It's too risky, Star. Too dangerous."

"I learned something from Pearl Chevalier. She told me she nearly died—she tripped down the stairs at her home and ended up in a life-threatening coma. Since then she does anything and everything 'risky'.

"I doubt you'd find Pearl Chevalier backpacking in third-world countries." This woman was incorrigible. "Marry me, Star. Stop faffing about and marry me." That was the last thing I thought would come out of my mouth, but it did, and I owned those words. I meant them.

She laughed. "Well that was romantic."

I laid my hand tentatively on her knee. The idea of any harm coming to her was like losing an arm, a leg. "Look, I just want to know you're safe. I can look after you. I love you, Star. I know I screwed up, but please give me a chance. I don't fuck around anymore. Seriously, I'm done with all that. I just want a normal life. I want you to be my wife."

"You're cute to say that, sweetie, but I've made up my mind. I need to see the world through the eyes of Diane Davis again, not Star Davis. I need this, Jake. I've been sober—without any pills or drink—for a month now. This is it for me. I can't go back to that shit. Ever. I need to turn my life around and backpacking around the world, soaking up foreign cultures where nobody knows who the hell I am, is my solution."

"When will you be back?"

"In a few months. The premiere for *Skye's The Limit* will probably be around July. I'll be back for that."

"There's nothing I can do then, to dissuade you?"

"Not a thing."

I bowed my head. Star was as stubborn as my father. I knew there was no point wasting my breath. "By the way, where did you learn to ride like that?"

"Didn't you watch all my movies before you hired me?" Then she laughed again, her wide smile stretching across her beautiful, happy face. "That's right, you *didn't* hire me! Bobby Duvall taught me how to ride when we did *The Trail*. He's a great horseman. I went to stay at his estate in Virginia once. I love Bobby so much."

"So what about this horse Max, then, when you go away?"

"He belongs to Pearl and Alexandre. Well, they've just sold him. I'm borrowing him for a few days before he goes to his forever home, here in Malibu."

"You can't go, Star. Please see reason."

"I'll write you," she said, as if that would appease me.

"Letters," I retorted. "No e-mails. Letters. I want to see your writing. Feel the paper in my hands."

"Deal," she promised. "I'm going to take a sabbatical from the Internet and cellphones, anyway."

"Shake on it? That you'll write me letters?"

"Sure," and she shook my hand, leaned in close and kissed me.

It was the most unexpected, treasured, magical kiss I'd ever experienced, hitting me hard in the gut.

Because something told me it would be her last.

15. Star

MINDY AND I had been gone a month. Apart from a German tourist staring into my eyes intently as we were sitting outside a restaurant in Bangkok one time, pretty much nobody recognized me. And if they did, with my short black pixie cut, I'd say, "I know, I know, I get it all the time—I wish. You think I'd be schlepping around with a backpack if I had Star Davis's megabucks?"

Every now and again, fed up with our simple accommodation, Mindy and I would splurge and hang out at a five star hotel. There's nothing like backpacking to make you appreciate the good things in life, like a basic hot shower.

We started our tour in Thailand, cut across to Laos, then took a boat down the Mekong River, crossing into Cambodia, where we were now.

When we got out of our little speedboat, which was basically a rowboat with a powerful engine, a little boy met us at the shore. "Welcome to the Kingdom of Cambodia," he said. Those simple words really struck me. I was in another land, another world, and it was thrilling.

And it was the most amazing, mind-freeing thing imaginable to be appreciated as just a person, not a movie star. In fact, Mindy was more popular than I was.

Now we were in Siem Reap, the home to Angkor Wat, one of the most famous religious monuments in the world, a ruin of the bygone Khmer Empire, once buried by jungle before it got "discovered" by a French explorer in the late 1800s, and then shut off for so many years by the Khmer Rouge, an extreme communist regime who practiced torture and genocide on anyone they considered "bourgeois" in the late 1970's. People talk about the horrors of Hitler and the Nazis (rightly so) but don't realize that what Pol Pot and his leaders did was right up there with the most vicious regimes in history. It was hard to imagine it happening so recently in history—the locals were so friendly. It was an eye-opener to see another world, another way of living, so far removed from who I was, and what I knew.

"Okay, so remind me, Star, why are we here?" Mindy asked, sipping fresh coconut water from a green coconut that a man had just hacked with a machete from a tree, ten minutes earlier (climbing the tree, no less). We were chilling out, taking a break from our tour of the temples.

I laughed. "Culture. To see what life is like outside the postage stamp that is LA. To discover the world, to know what it's like to be normal."

Mindy held my hand and looked at me with her Bambi eyes, her pretty round face deadly serious. "Star, you will never be normal."

"Hey, I'm trying."

"It's all good," Mindy said, "but I had no idea how tough this would be. Cold showers, weird food. I miss home."

"Don't be a pussy," I said, "we need to see this

through."

"What are you trying to prove, Star?"

"That I'm not a 'mollycoddled, Cristal-drinking brat' as Jake once called me when we were filming our first day."

"What the hell does 'mollycoddled' mean?"

"I have no idea, ask him."

"So this whole hard-ass trip is basically to prove something to Jake Wild?"

I shrugged. "Maybe."

"What *is* it with you two? Why can't you just call it a day and stop playing games?"

"Because we both have some growing up to do first. If we hook up again? Right now? We'd probably destroy each other."

"Okay, I get that, both of you being so . . . volatile. But still, it seems like you're wasting precious time. What if he meets someone else while you're traveling?"

"Then it wasn't meant to be."

"How can you be so cool about it? If I were crazy about a guy, I'd be too scared to lose him."

"Who says I'm crazy about him? Anyway, *'What's for you won't go against you.'* "

"Who said that?"

"Pearl Chevalier. Her grandmother—or someone wise—told her that."

"Pearl, your new *mentor*?" Mindy said, with a tiny trace of jealousy in her tone.

"She's cool. I thought she was this perfect woman, but in fact, she had a pretty screwed up past and managed to really make her personal life work, so it gives me hope. Hope that I too can lead a normal life."

Mindy rolled her eyes. "You think that being married to a sexy French multi-billionaire who hasn't even turned thirty yet, is *normal*?" She laughed. "I love you, Star. It's all, 'Angie this, and Brad that.' Honey, you are on another *planet* and the sooner you realize that you—and your life—is different, and actually quite freaky compared to most mortal beings, and stop playing this 'normal' game, the easier things will be for you."

"You think?"

She drained her coconut, making slurping noises with the straw. "Let's go and see Angkor Wat."

"But they say the best time to visit is five a.m."

"That's why we need to go now," she suggested. "Do the opposite of what the guidebooks say. It's almost sunset. If we go now it'll be half empty. We go tomorrow, early? it'll be like Grand Central Station."

"Or we could go to Bayon with the heads carved into the stone, or Ta Prohm, the Tomb Raider Temple where they shot the movie."

"Good idea, then you can tell your buddy *Angelina*."

We got up from our seats by the little roadside shack and gathered our electric bicycles, and set off on another adventure. A whole family, packed on a motorcycle—their clothing a patchwork of vibrant pinks and yellows—zipped past: mom, dad, a little boy and his sister, waving frantically, smiling big toothy smiles. An elephant and his master sauntered by, the great creature plodding lazily along, its long eyelashes blinking thoughtfully—its tail swishing off flies.

I looked at Mindy and grinned. "We're in Cambodia! Check that scene out. And listen! There are monkeys squawking in the forest over there, can't you hear them? Now please don't tell me you feel homesick, Mindy."

"You're right," she said, and hopped on her bike. "This is freakin' *awesome*!"

Lara Croft's temple complex was beautiful, partly because it was half ruinous, with giant Banyon trees taking over, clawing their talons into the ancient edifices. I loved being an anonymous tourist in this faraway land. Nobody fussing over me, no one having a clue who I was, or how much money I made.

Just an ordinary girl on the trip of a lifetime.

PRODUCTION
Shining Star

DIRECTOR
Jake Wild

DATE
May

SCENE
Star's letter

TAKE
16

CAMERA
Jake Wild

I HAD JUST finished reading a new script that I'd fallen in love with, about a young blind woman (having nobody in mind but Star to play the role), when my mail arrived. Each day the postwoman had come my heart leapt, then sank again when there was no news from Star. She had broken her promise. No e-mails, either, no text messages. She really had checked out. I didn't have a clue where she was, nor did her agent, nor the Chevaliers (who always seemed to know everything). Or if they did, they weren't letting on. Bizarrely, the only person who had heard from her was Brian. A text, like clockwork, would arrive once a week, which always said pretty much the same thing:

We are alive and well, know you'll spread the word, please don't worry.

She knew what a gossip Brian was, I guessed, and that news would filter through.

Today, though, a letter, with colorful stamps pasted all over it from Zambia—my favorite being a hare with a lion in the background, which looked as if it was based on some fable or folkloric tale as it was called Kalulu and the Lion—was waiting for me in my mailbox. I smelled the envelope, trying to inhale some sort of trace of Star, any hope of her—anything to feel her closer.

Fierce was as excited as I was, bounding next to me as I went out into the kitchen to get a knife to open it.

"You want a sniff, Fierce?" I said, ridiculously offering him the envelope "no drooling though." He whimpered as if he could smell her fingertips sealing the letter closed. "I know, we miss her badly, don't we?"

I carefully opened the slightly crumpled envelope. Once, when I was small, I ripped a letter from my mother open with my bare thumb, and was screamed at by my anally retentive dad for being "slovenly". My tidy habits were a tribute to him, although I didn't see my obsessive-compulsive neatness as positive, but rather, as a negative trait.

Star was messy; threw her clothes around, chucked off her shoes at the end of the day so they lay here, there and everywhere, haphazardly on the floor. Things in disordered piles. At the time, I admonished her for it, but all I craved now was her beautiful chaos surrounding me at every turn.

She was like an exotic butterfly that couldn't be caught; elusive, mystical. Had she met someone on her worldwide travels? Was she going to come back with a goddamn ring on her finger?

I pulled out the letter, which was two pages long, written in crayon on both sides, in large, quite school-girlish handwriting.

Dearest Jake,

I'm sorry I haven't written - well I have

actually, a few times, except I never got it together to go to a post office. When I see you, I'll hand over a few dog-eared letters, half written. For now, this will be my official letter.

Uh-oh . . was this about to be bad news? Was she going to tell me she'd met the man of her dreams? Some hippy she'd met at the Taj Mahal, or something? Or a Bollywood actor from Mumbai?

Mindy and I are now in Zambia helping out at an elephant orphanage. Yeah, I know, Zambia's a long way from South East Asia. She fell in love with a vet and animal rights activist named David, who we met in Vietnam (you know they eat dogs in Vietnam?) who happened to be there temporarily.

As you know, Mindy hadn't dated in years, so meeting this man is very exciting for her. He's a cool guy, really dedicated to his job. He has a mobile veterinary unit, which basically means he flies a little plane to reach out of the way areas of the bush. We all fantasize about saving the world, don't we? Well, he really is saving the world, on a daily basis. His job is both heart-warming and heartbreaking.

Do you remember how Mindy was kind of out of shape? Not anymore. A couple of stomach bugs and being in love slimmed her down in record time. It's so wonderful to see my best, and oldest friend, find true love.

Anyway, it's a long story, but David invited us (well, Mindy) here to the Elephant Orphanage Project. As you know, with the obsession that many Chinese have about aphrodisiac "medicines" elephants are being decimated for their tusks, more than ever. I always wonder who these monsters are, don't you? Some fat CEO sitting behind his desk in Beijing with a walnut penis, thinking that slaughtered and massacred elephants will be the answer to his erectile dysfunction, with a mistress who probably finds him repulsive anyway, who's only with him for the money, and a wife who gave up long ago, and whose only pleasure is her children.

Did you know that one elephant is killed every 15 minutes? That means that if this continues, no elephant will be alive by 2025.

Trust Star to tell it like it is, I thought. I read on:

Anyway, enough of my rant. Baby elephants are brought here. Many of them have seen their parents slaughtered in front of them. As you know, elephants actually shed tears and have a memory. Like humans, they are emotional. Every time a member of their family dies they grieve deeply. They have an amazing sense of family and are herd animals, so the babies have bonded together and are very close. They also become extremely attached to their keepers. Did you know that cows' milk can kill a toddler elephant? It took years to develop the special elephant milk formula, which they are fed with a bottle, just like a human baby. It's the cutest thing you've ever seen.

When the calves arrive at the nursery they are given a name that reflects their circumstance and story. A new one came in the other day (I can't pronounce his name but it means "symbol of hope"), who was found mourning his mom. The Zambian Wildlife Authority heard a gunshot and when they arrived, the poachers were hacking the tusks out of the mother's face, the little calf standing nearby.

Only thirty years ago there were three million elephants and now it's down to a piddly 272,000. How sad is that?

Before Pearl Chevalier got married

to Alexandre she was a documentary producer working for Haslit Films. She'll be coming out to visit us here as she wants to cover this-yeah, I think making Hollywood movies pales in comparison; she knows where her priorities lie.

Uh, oh, I thought. This is the end of Star's acting career.

Don't worry, Jake. I know I can do more good by appearing in People Magazine, talking about topics like this, than staying here working. I've spoken to Angelina about her amazing humanitarian efforts - she's my role model. The more successful my movies, and the more famous I am, the more attention I can draw to the bad there is in the world.

On a personal level? I miss you. A lot. I've been thinking so much about who I am, what my purpose on this planet is, about you, about Leo. He and I went through something horrific together so obviously we bonded. He was a very special person and even thinking about him brings tears to my eyes.

I needed this time to reflect on everything that happened. I beat myself up a lot about slipping back into my old addictive ways. I needed to forgive myself, take some time away to heal. But I miss working with you. I miss our camaraderie. We have so many things in common, Jake. What is it about you that makes me know that you belong to me and nobody else? You're mine, Jake, and as far as I am capable of belonging to anybody, I do belong to you.

Yours,

Star

It was as if a hummingbird had been set free in my ribcage when I read that last paragraph of Star's letter. "You're mine." Tears sprung to my eyes. How could a woman have this much of a hold on me? How was it possible that I felt that my life was a vacuum without her? I didn't *want* to feel this way. I had fought for so long against this emotion that was consuming me to the point of obsession. But I simply couldn't bear it any longer.

I'd had enough of her independence game. This was crazy! *Why* were we apart from each other? Right from the second we'd set eyes on one another, at the read-through for *Skye's The Limit*, it was obvious we were in love. Yes, it *was* love at first sight, but neither of us trusted it to be true. Neither of us trusted *ourselves* to be capable of a normal relationship. And maybe a "normal" relationship will never be possible for us, ever. But who the fuck gets to judge what "normal" is anyway? Two screwed-up Hollywood misfits—the pair of us. And so what? Did that mean we couldn't find our own little quirky paradise with each other?

It was time for us to be united, once and for all. And I wasn't going to take no for an answer. I kissed the letter and carefully put it back in its envelope.

Tomorrow I was getting on a plane to Zambia.

Enough was bloody well enough.

I WAS DRENCHED. We'd been giving the elephants a good scrub down in their watering hole, which they adored. Their favorite game was to spray us with their twisty trunks that were almost like creatures unto themselves.

You know when you have that feeling that someone is watching you? Well someone was:

I looked up and saw a figure in the distance. At first I thought it was David, coming back from a trip from Botswana—he'd been away for a week now, leaving Mindy and me at the camp. But it wasn't David.

It was Jake. I shrieked with excitement, and

took steps to race toward him, but the oozy mud squelched around my sneakers and I was sucked further into the sludge. I fell flat on my face in a kind of belly-flop. As I came up spluttering, I got another elephant spray from Nkala, the baby calf I'd been scrubbing with a big loofa. I could hear Jake chuckling, and I too roared with laughter.

"Got any dark chocolate?" I shouted out at him.

"I fly halfway around the world to see you and you're asking for chocolate?"

I managed to extricate myself from the muddy water and splashed my way into his arms. We pressed ourselves into each other, me a blubbering wreck as I buried my face into his chest. He smelled of sun and mint and freshly laundered T-shirt.

"I almost didn't recognize you," he said. "With that funny hair of yours."

"I told you . . ." I sniveled—not understanding why I felt so emotional—"it would be a good disguise."

"What's with the tears?" He cupped his hand on my jaw, tipped up my chin and took in the vision of my dirty face. I was bronzed from the strong sun, a few freckles on my nose, my eyelashes soaked with crying. "All because you think I didn't bring chocolate?"

"Because I missed you and thought you had better things to do than miss me back," I said.

"I'll always miss you back, Star. Always."

Jake told me about his plan to take me away from the camp on a sort of honeymoon. At least that's the way it seemed to me after my simple life, sleeping on a makeshift camp bed and taking lukewarm showers. The trip was to be a surprise; I had no idea where we'd be going.

"A sort of safari," he told me, giving me a clue. "But first to the largest sheet of falling water in the world."

"Let me guess, Victoria Falls?"

"That's right."

Jake pulled out a 1960's guide book from his pocket that had belonged to his granddad: "The snow-white sheet seemed like myriads of small comets rushing on in one direction, each of which left behind its nucleus rays of foam . . . the most wonderful sight I had witnessed in Africa."

"Who said that?" I asked.

"David Livingstone, supposedly the first westerner to set eyes on Victoria Falls in 1855. And we'll be paying him homage tonight. I've hired the Royal Livingstone Express, an old-fashioned steam train that's still in operation for tourists. Except we have the whole train to ourselves for dinner this evening. We can go back in time. Back to the 1930s when it was built."

I looked down at my shorts and muddy knees. "I think in the olden days the ladies would have looked like ladies when they boarded a smart train for dinner."

"I have a car waiting. And packed in the trunk some Louis Vuitton suitcases full of beautiful clothing, fit for the most exquisite of all ladies."

"You brought me clothes?"

"The advantage of being a successful director is you get to work with the best costume designers in the world, you know every single measurement of your leading lady. No prison uniform this time. I had Edith make you a set of outfits that would make Daisy Buchanan envious. Get in the car—you can shower and dress at the hotel."

FROM THIS MOMENT ON, I entered into a new world of pure, decadent luxury, having somehow forgotten that I could live this way if I wanted to, pretty much every day of the year—at least when I wasn't filming. I'd quite disregarded the fact I was a movie star, but Jake reminded me, because he was treating me like a princess. No . . . a queen.

The train was beautiful: a shiny, old-fashioned locomotive, painted in red, black, and gold, and inside all gleaming teak wood and shiny brass. I felt like I'd stepped into an Agatha Christie novel.

We sipped virgin cocktails as we watched the stunning African scenery move by, entering Mosi-oa-Tunya Game Park at a snail's pace. We saw a couple of giraffes calmly sauntering by the train, monkeys, and zebra.

Our dinner was a five-course meal, although my appetite was small because I was so excited to be with Jake, I could hardly eat. My dress was low at the neckline, sleeveless and cut on the bias—no zip, no fastenings, just a silky, streamline satin in emerald green, that looked great with my jet-black hair. Jake was wearing a tux, but Californian style, his shirt unbuttoned, no tie. His hair disheveled and messy. Neither of us ate much, just stared at each other—me giggling nervously when he nodded to our waiter to leave us be.

I knew what was coming, and although it sent goose pimples rippling across my arms and thighs, my heart was racing.

I relaxed back into a sumptuous red velvet couch, twilight shading and lighting my face in sharp chiaroscuro shadows, as we listened to the bush birds goodnight chatter, and observed swathes of purple wash across the dark pink sky like a pastel drawing; surreal in its boldness of color and form. It was pure magic.

Jake put his hand on my calf and caressed my ankle, lifting it up onto his knee. He slowly undid the strap of my high-heeled sandal. Just his touch, the stroke of his fingers sent a bolt of desire straight to the apex of my thighs.

I hadn't expected this. So soon. So powerful. I guessed it was the unintended roller coaster ride we had unwittingly embarked on a year ago—the gamut of emotions we had put each other through, and now we were alone, lost in our thoughts of each other, and nothing more. He didn't speak. Nor did I. There was such intensity that danced between us; invisible but almost tangible.

He lifted my ankle to his lips and whispered kisses up along my calf. His hand rose higher, stroking the silkiness of my inner thigh. A low moan rumbled in his throat as if I were one of the wildebeests outside in the bush, and he the lion. I was his dinner; our five-course meal—that he had hardly touched—had been his appetizer. A typical Leo—hence his lion tattoo on his bicep.

His hand rose higher. I squirmed lower into the sofa.

"What if someone comes in?"

"They won't. Strict instructions," he said. I relaxed and gave myself over even more. His fingers walked higher up my thigh and found my wetness. Waiting. Wanton.

"Fuck. No knickers."

"No."

"For me?"

"No. Panties break the line."

"The line of your sexy arse?"

"Yes. A tip I learned from Marilyn Monroe. Never break the line."

"But you knew I'd be exploring you here, didn't you?"

"Yes."

"So no panties is also to please me, isn't it?"

"No," I lied, my poker face not flinching.

"You like to drive me crazy, don't you, Star?"

"Yes I do."

"Why?"

"Because I want you desperate for me."

He narrowed his eyes.

"So you'll never, ever want anyone else. So you'll always be afraid of losing me."

"You're cruel," he said, thrusting his finger into me. "Fuck, you're wet. Fuck, you make me hard. Your wet pussy must be ruining your dress."

"Probably," I said.

"I need to clean you up then." He pulled me towards him and rolled my dress up my thighs, above my hips. He stared at me there for a long time, licking his lips.

I enjoyed being his prey. I flicked my eyes out of the window and fancied I saw a lion in the distance, in the dark of night. I turned my attention back to Jake, a different kind of lion. He was biting his lower lip hard. In preparation. He drilled his eyes into mine. "Has anyone else tasted this?"

"Maybe," I taunted.

He knew I was kidding but said, "This. Is. Fucking. Well. Mine. I swear I'd be capable of killing any man who tried to come between us."

His jealousy was making my nipples harden. I rolled my hips so his fingers squelched deeper inside me. "I don't think they'd dare. Your lion tattoo would frighten them off," I teased.

"Don't joke, Star. It's not funny." He swept his tongue up and down my soaked slit, groaning as he sucked in my juices. "You're mine. You're fucking well mine," he murmured into my pussy, "please tell me this is all mine."

One of my dreams flashed before me. Hadn't Leo said things like that to me? Interesting that my imagination was coming true, but in a different way. I tipped a little smile at Jake and acquiesced.

Poor guy deserved to know for sure. "I'm yours. No other man has gone this far."

He growled into me in appreciation at what I'd said. "Fuck my mouth, baby," he murmured.

I began to rock my hips back and forth as his tongue flickered on my clit. Then he carried on where we'd left off in London. He seized my ass in one hand, his thumb pressing my pussy, while his middle finger—lubricated from my arousal—entered my ass, finding it's way inside—little by little. His finger, his thumb, and his tongue, the rumbling motion and vibration of the steam train—all joined in a beautiful, sexual symphony, concentrated in this small area that was now my universe. As if that wasn't enough—which it most certainly was—his other hand played with my nipple. Another push to my clit and I was history. "Coming like a train," I could have said if I'd had the words, but all I could do was cry out, my orgasm crashing through me in an almost violent wave.

It was official:

I was in love with Jake Wild.

PRODUCTION
Shining Star

DIRECTOR
- Jake Wild

DATE
May

SCENE
Devil's Rod

TAKE
18

CAMERA
- Jake Wild

I WAS PULLING out all the stops to win Star over. I still hadn't fucked her yet, though. In my mind, she was still my virgin. What happened in London hadn't happened. It was too much of a fuck-up to bear. On both our parts. We needed a clean slate and this African trip was it.

The train ride was exotic and perfect in every way, and although Star wanted more, I wouldn't give it to her. Not yet. We slept together at the hotel that night, holding hands, wrapped about each other like mantels, so when we awoke the next day, early, we felt like awe-struck teenagers.

All the more in love with each other.

I took her to Victoria Falls.

First we hiked along the top, observing the churning waters of the Zambezi River and the curtain of mist that gave the falls its Zambian name, *Mosi-oa-Tunya*, or the "Smoke that Thunders." We very carefully picked our way down the side and along the gorge facing the drop. Sunlight refracted off the moving sheet of water, causing rainbows to arc through the misty spray. The noise was deafening with the violent churning, thundering below us.

"Over five hundred million tons of water plummet per minute to the drop a hundred meters below," I told Star. "That's three thousand cubic meters per second. The columns of spray can be seen from literally miles away."

"What's that in my language?" Star asked, her fingers hooked into the waistband of my jeans to balance herself, or to bring me down with her if she fell. Either way, we were in this together. "We Yankees don't think in cubic meters."

"A hundred and twenty million gallons of water roaring down into the gorge every minute.

It's twice as high as the Niagara Falls. It's over a mile wide. Isn't that incredible?"

"Wow."

"Yeah, wow."

We both laughed.

"We're going for a swim." I told her. "At the very *very* top of the falls, and we're going to be only one meter away from the drop."

"Yeah, right."

"You watch," I said. "It's called Devil's Pool. Come, our guide's waiting. I've brought our swimsuits."

OUR GUIDE DID a back somersault, his toes plunging into the water of Devil's Pool, the pool of water at the summit of Victoria Falls, before it cascades and crashes onto rocks, three hundred feet below. It seemed like a crazy, death defying act, and Star and I watched in horror. I was convinced he'd be washed over the edge with the force of the current, but when he came up for air, he stood there grinning.

"Come," he beckoned.

Star and I looked at each other, in a "like, seriously?" sort of way, counted to three, and jumped in holding hands, feeling that our lives could all be over in seconds, but surprised when our heads bobbed up above water, and that we hadn't been washed over the edge like a couple of Pooh sticks. We laughed triumphantly and swam over to our guide, who was standing less than a meter away from the edge, by a natural ridge, just before the mammoth drop of the waterfall.

"Are you sure it's safe to go that close?" I asked, the whirl of water swirling around me in an eddy, cooling the adrenaline coursing through my veins.

"Let's do it," Star said, swimming over towards the mighty thunder. I followed her. If she was going to plunder over the edge to her death, I wanted to go with her.

We reached the ledge and our guide (whose name was Alpha-Omega!) said, "I'll hold your legs and you can hang over."

"In for a penny, in for a pound," I said, my

heart thundering. Letting him take hold of my ankles, I peered into the roaring misty spray. We were definitely dare-devilishly crazy to be doing this, no question. But then Star and I thrived on crazy. Crazy was in our DNA.

It was her turn next. Just for good measure, I too, gripped her ankles. I'd been waiting for Star all my life, and I didn't want to lose her now.

SOMETHING ABOUT risking your life brings you more alive than ever. I mean, not that hanging over Victoria Falls—the largest waterfall on the planet—is statistically more dangerous than getting into a car (far less so), but still, it sure as hell got the blood flowing.

So when Star and I sat in the garden of our luxurious house that I'd rented: the Chongwe River House on the lower Zambezi, watching the sun set, I felt that life simply couldn't get any better. We had defied death and laughed in its face, and now we were here.

The Chongwe River House looked like a luxurious version of Fred Flintstone's abode, situated on the banks of the magical Chongwe River, a tributary of the Zambezi, with a stunning view of the dramatic mountainous scenery beyond. Many animals come to the Chongwe River to drink, and as Star and I took in our breathtaking surroundings from the deck, I knew that my choice to come here in "rustic luxury" was a wise one. The game-viewing was superlative, even right from our open living room, and from the bedrooms too—we were almost at one with the wildlife outdoors. The lodge mimicked an animal's riverbank lair, entwined with tree roots, mud and rocks, but super-luxurious, and we had a team of staff administering to our every whim.

Soon after we arrived, a herd of elephants ambled towards the banks of the river to drink, and warthogs scurried about in the back yard like they were house pets. Monkeys too. When we went for a swim in the pool, some hippos also went for a dip, right below us, wallowing in the river.

We had all sorts of activities planned over the

next few days: canoe trips on the river, jeep game drives, picnics in the bush, night feast barbeques, and photography excursions to shoot (with our lenses only) the majesty of these incredible animals in their habitat. But for now, the only thing that was holding my attention one hundred percent was the most beautiful and perfect specimen of mammal on earth:

Star Davis.

19.
Star

J AKE AND I had a "waterfall shower" in the beautiful bathroom next to our bedroom, after having taken in our fill of wildlife for the night, while watching the streaky orange and purple sky fill the horizon, and now, I knew that a very special moment was next on our agenda.

And it terrified me.

The "deed" was done in London. But when you're pumped full of prescription drugs as I was (hey, drugs are drugs even if they do come in a vial with your name on them), your memory is one hazy, slurry mess.

What do I remember about that night?

(a) That Jake Wild could make me come, even

in my sorry state, and . . .

(b) Jake Wild left me wanting more, and . . .

(c) We both needed therapy, and . . .

(d) We won joint prize for fucked-up-ness.

We were outside on the veranda, enclosed in our bed, surrounded by the gauzy mosquito net, listening to the croaking of frogs and the groaning of lions—at least that's what it sounded like. Who knew? Maybe it was a prowling leopard, but once again, we were living on the edge. The edge of the biggest waterfall in the world, the edge of the most beautiful horizon in the world. Jake and I didn't do things by halves. We tortured each other, we devoured each other's souls.

We breathed for one another.

Jake and me. Me and Jake. Where had I heard that before?

We were one. He was my *media naranja*—Pearl had been right. So I guess we *did* do things by halves. Two halves making one whole.

"Let me stare at you," I said, eating up my view. He was truly exquisite. He looked like a character in a Jane Austen or Bronte novel . . .

which hero, or anti-hero, I couldn't work out yet. Darcy? With that smattering of arrogance and moodiness, fine-tuned with sensibility and vulnerability? No, Jake was too unpredictable. Heathcliff? No, because in the end, Heathcliff was an asshole, mainly because he was cruel to dogs. But there was something outer-worldly about Jake, although I couldn't put my finger on it.

He was the one to speak first. "You're breathtakingly beautiful, Star."

"Even with my short black hair?"

"Especially with your short black hair. You could be bald and you'd still be beautiful."

I giggled. I was as nervous as a schoolgirl.

"I had to stop myself from ravaging you last night on the train. When you came for me—for us—you . . . you undid me."

"You undid *me*," I said.

He was kneeling on the bed, his chest bare but his pants still on. My gaze traced the contours of his lean, firm thighs, the bulge at his crotch, his rock-hard biceps; notably, his left arm where his lion lived, the corded muscles in his forearms that had become that way by carrying heavy cameras around, he once told me. I looked back to his eyes; dark not just with lust, but brimming with love: a deadly combination, because I knew that this was it—there was no return.

I laid my hand on his groin, I was also kneeling on the bed. "You're imprisoned here, let me help you."

He inhaled a sharp breath but didn't exhale again. I unbuttoned his jeans, one button at a time, savoring the feel of the solidity beneath. A low rumble emanated from his throat, and a tiny muscle in his jaw clenched; a muscle I hadn't noticed before. I pulled his pants over his firm thighs, and slipped his boxer briefs down his legs. Then he let out a long sigh. His cock sprang up and a crooked smile teased my lips. I could hang a coat on that, I thought—so powerful, so solid.

I had never studied him before. Not like this— in a quiet, restful way, with all the time in the world. Before, we had been frantic, fearful, and selfish. Not trusting one another.

"Your cock is beautiful," I whispered, as if the elephants and wild creatures might hear. "Truly magnificent. It's a work of fucking art." I placed my finger on that fine, wispy hairline from his bellybutton down, trailing my touch to the tip of his smooth, soft crown. He groaned. His huge erection flexed, alive to my feathery stroke. I traced my finger down further, along the velvety ridge, down, down, and cupped his balls gently in my hand.

"Fuck, you're amazing," he said, his eyes hooded. "You're my queen."

"And you're my king. My Lion King."

Suddenly, he grabbed my wrist, then the other, and in one swift, unexpected movement handcuffed both together in one of his large hands, drawing them above my head—as if my touch had been slow torture, my hands now his prisoners. His dominance made my stomach free fall, like I was on the Great Dipper at a fairground.

"What are you going to do to me?"

"Everything," he breathed into my mouth, holding my jaw with his free hand.

His lips hovered over mine and my tongue peaked out. I could feel wetness pooling between my legs—not being allowed to touch him made me feel hopelessly vulnerable, but also spiked with a rush of lust.

He pulled back so he could focus on my eyes—our gazes fused together. Now it was his turn to study me. His look was dark, almost frightening—carnal desire mixed with a strange sort of empathy, as if he felt badly for me in some way.

"There's no turning back after this, Star. Is this what you want?"

Are you crazy? "Yeah, it's what I want."

"Do you realize what you're getting into with me?"

"Maybe," I teased. *Yeah, I know.*

"If I give you my all, I'll own your heart."

Arrogant bastard, I thought. He took my lower lip between his teeth and pulled gently. "And you'll own mine," he added. *Oh, okay.*

"And I'll own this," he said, his hand trailing down to my soaked center as he traced his finger up and down my slit. He pressed my clit as if it were a button and I whimpered, bucking my hips at him. "And this will get hooked on my cock, like a drug." Then he slipped a finger into my wet hole. "And this. You'll get addicted and want me to fuck you the whole time."

"Yeah," I whispered, my breath light on his lips. "I can cope with that." His words sounded familiar as if I'd heard them before. *Déja-vu.*

"And I'm jealous. Possessive. Intense. And I like to fuck. A lot. Can you handle that?"

"As long as it's only me," I said, sighing into his lips, his conversation scaring me a little.

"You bet it'll only be you. Because since I got a sample of this tight little pussy in London?" His finger dipped deeper inside me, illustrating his words, "I don't want anything else, I can't think of anything else."

"Good," I said.

"Good," he echoed, extracting his finger from inside me and then popping it in his mouth.

I couldn't contain the little smirk that was shyly quivering on my lips. I tried to bite it away.

"What?" he said, still holding my wrists above my head with his other hand.

Sex Addict meets Attention Junkie. The perfect match. "Nothing," I answered. "Just shut the fuck up and kiss me."

In a heartbeat his lips melded to mine. Our

tongues darted out to meet each other, and he held my jaw with his free hand, so my lips were his prisoners as well as my wrists. He licked my tongue up and down, and then flickered his tongue on my lips. Then he let go of my chin and fisted his cock, steering it up and down my wet cleft. Oh fuck, I remembered this torturous pleasure in the shower. Teasing me to oblivion.

"Please," I whimpered.

"That's right, Star, tell me what you want."

"I want you to fuck me."

"I can't hear you, baby, what is it you want?"

"I want your big cock inside me—I want you to fuck me," I moaned louder, our eyes connected. "And I want to touch you."

He groaned, let go of my wrists, and I sighed with relief. I shook them out and grabbed handfuls of his dark blond, mussed-up hair, the back of his neck damp with perspiration. I could smell him. Musky. Sex and desire—an almost imperceptible odor, but I could smell it on his skin.

We were still on our knees. I grabbed his biceps to give me purchase as I slipped under him and opened my legs wide. "Fuck me, Jake. Please."

My eyes lifted to the sight of his glorious erection and I was momentarily distracted from my mission. Yes, I wanted him to fuck me, but I also wanted him in my mouth first. But he carefully edged his body down, his elbows planted on either side of my shoulders, so his weight was hovering over me but not pressing down.

The tip of his erection was poised at my opening. I writhed beneath him. He entered a millimeter.

"Oh, God," I cried out.

He started to fuck me, but only an inch inside. In and out, just his wide crest teasing every sensitive nerve ending. I was drenched. "Please," I moaned. "More."

But then he started the teasing assault on my clit, fucking it. I was practically doing the splits my legs were so wide open, willing him to ram me hard; enter in as deep as he could. He cupped my bottom, holding it close to him, his rhythm, from clit to inside me changing without warning, but never going in very far. My fingers were digging into his back, then clawing his taut ass, trying to draw his muscular butt into me, but he was too strong for me to control. I could hear my ragged breath, my begging words as he continued his tease.

"I love you, Star. You're my life."

My tongue tangled with his, lashing out in more ways than one. For the first time ever I didn't care to hear his words; I wanted his body, every last inch of it, with none to spare. "Shut up talking—and put your money where your mouth is," I ordered, the Star Davis brat wanting it all *now, now, now.* I sucked at his tongue, drawing it inside my mouth to show him just how deep he needed to enter. That did it.

With one powerful thrust he plunged inside me on a throaty growl. But then stilled, his size filling me up completely. "I'm sorry, baby, are you alright?"

This alien feeling was not what I had expected. Jake was right; there was no going back. We were one: Dracula with his fangs, an elephant with his tusks, an airplane with wings. Jake and I were a part of each other now. A tear slid down my cheek. I belonged to someone else and it shocked me. I hadn't considered the implications of this physical union. I could feel his huge member throbbing inside me. I had been invaded. Both my body, and my mind.

Jake kissed my teary eye. "I love you, Star. Forever."

"I love you back," I whispered, holding the pain of him inside me. This *thing* that had undone my independence. This serpent—literally a serpent—tempting me with the fruit. Right now, I resented Jake. I hated him because I felt weak. The "weaker vessel" as women had been described in literature. The truth fucking well hurt.

He pulled out slowly, just the tip of him resting at my entrance once more. We lay that way a while, the new me in a quandary. I wanted to push him away, lash out at him, pummel his head, sink my teeth into his face.

I hated him.

Because I had fallen so hard. I had no control over the emotions spiraling through my female body.

He held my face like it was the most delicate, breakable object in the world. He kissed the tip of my nose, my eyes, he breathed in my hair. I felt that familiar spark, again, light between my thighs. I hooked my calves around his legs and pushed my hips at him a fraction. He entered me, just a tiny way. Fucking me slowly. Fucking me gently, his eyes never leaving mine, his breath on my lips. Soon his rhythm had me wanting more and I relaxed, giving myself over, acquiescing to my newfound womanhood.

This new status quo sucked.

But it also fucking rocked.

I AWOKE A FEW hours later, our bodies entangled; Jake's legs draped over me, his arms wrapped around me in a vice. I nuzzled my nose into his golden skin, running it up and down his chest, burying my face into his scent.

Jake's prophecy was right. I wanted more of this drug. I unhooked myself, my tongue trailing up and down his sleepy torso, his steady breathing in my ear. I unraveled his arms and rolled him on his back. He moaned in his heavy slumber. I drank in my view, visible because of the early dawn light; his abs, divided into segments like a Roman warrior, and I dragged my gaze up to his beautiful face—the straight, unyielding nose, the high cheekbones, the strong jawline. I pressed my finger lightly on the spot there, where I'd noticed a tiny muscle pulse earlier that day, and smiled to myself. I liked the fact that I got even the miniscule muscles on his face riled up. Me, Star: the dysfunctional Hollywood casualty had found true love. With this equally troubled man.

My *media naranja.*

My eyes wandered to his fine, solid legs, his smooth skin, then skimmed back to the part that had the addict in me wanting another fix. I began to stroke him there. His dick moved, but his eyes were still closed. I pushed his thighs apart and slipped my body between them. I edged my way down the mattress and rested my chin between the junction of his thighs. I flicked my tongue lazily at his balls, then swirled it around in circles. I heard a low moan rumble through his lithe, golden body. Did I dare wake the sleeping lion?

I took his balls in my mouth and sucked

gently.

"Oh, fuck, am I dreaming?"

"No," I mumbled incoherently, balls in mouth. "This is no dream."

His cock throbbed, hardening by the second. Just the thought of it was making me wet. I swept my tongue up and down his length and within seconds he was a hard, unrelenting rod. I looked up at him, a lascivious gleam in my eye.

"I love it when you suck my cock," he murmured. "Oh fuck, Star."

I took all of him in my mouth, and fisted the root of his dick tightly between my grip. But the truth was, all this I was doing for my greedy self, not him. I mounted him, poising his erection in the perfect position so all I had to do was plunge down onto it. His eyes flew wide open.

"Oh baby, you're going to undo me completely."

His strong arms wrapped around me, his hands on my hips, controlling the tempo. I thrust my breasts forward so he'd take my nipple in his mouth, which he did, sucking at it, pulling my teat so I was seeing flashing lights behind my closed eyes. An invisible thread was connecting all my pleasure zones as I continued to pump him, his size ripping through me, meeting me with his thrusts, which were stroking all the right places, and a new spot deep inside me that I had discovered a few hours earlier that was driving me crazy with desire.

I held his head in my hands as I fucked him, harder and harder, aroused by his groaning and threats to come if I didn't slow down. The tendons in his neck pulsed, sweat glistened on his brow. The tip of his hard cock was rubbing that sacred little space of mine, over and over. I felt the build, like climbing a mountain when you reach the summit, and I detonated on top of him, crying out with pleasure, my climax overtaking every hormone, every cell in my emptied body. Jake came too, simultaneously, my visible and audible ecstasy turning him on so much that it was like pressing a button. This was our fourth round in one night and the sun hadn't even risen yet.

Jake Wild: my new drug on tap.

PRODUCTION
Shining Star

DIRECTOR
Jake Wild

DATE
Winter

SCENE
Elephant memory

TAKE
20

CAMERA
Jake Wild

I HAD PERSUADED STAR to move in with me. She sold her house in Hancock Park, because the memory of her last time there was too awful to bear. It was jinxed, she decided, so didn't ever step inside again. We were looking for a place to buy together. Meanwhile, she said she felt at home here on Sunset Boulevard.

My next mission was marrying her, but in true stubborn-Star-fashion she assured me that she would never marry. Not me, not anyone. I knew why. She didn't like the feeling of losing control. She had already turned into a sex fiend, wanting it every day, sometimes several times. I sure as hell wasn't complaining, but if she was like most normal women, I knew her appetite would wane. But by marrying me, I think she felt I'd hold all the cards if we were married, and being Star Davis, that didn't sit well with her.

But I wanted to stick a ring on that elegant finger of hers ASAP.

Summer came and went, the movie premiere of *Skye's The Limit* took place at Leicester Square in London and was a massive hit. Kate Middleton publically declared Star her favorite actress and even invited us over to the Palace for dinner. Star was more famous than ever, so when the Oscar nominations were announced, I wasn't surprised when she was chosen as one of the five contenders for Best Actress in a Leading Role. Meryl had also received a nomination for Best Supporting Actress (surprise, surprise), and Pearl Chevalier and the producers, Brian included, for Best Picture. And yours truly? I too was nominated. For Best Director.

Meanwhile, Star and I had begun rehearsals for my theatre production in the West End—the story about the blind girl—Star with the leading role. I'd been worried, at first, that being together twenty-four seven would be overkill, but her professionalism never let that get in the way. We were able to disassociate ourselves from home life and shift full gear into work mode. It worked.

Her brother Travis was put on trial and charged for voluntary manslaughter, kidnapping, and obstructing the course of justice. Star had to testify against him, which despite their history, was hard on her. But she had no choice. By freeing Leo of all blame, she had to tell the truth. Travis got fifteen years, but we all knew that with good behavior he'd be out sooner. Leo was proven unequivocally innocent, and Janice let off with "reasonable doubt" as to her involvement, although Star didn't want anything more to do with her. How could she? Their whole relationship had been a lie. Janice sneaked off to a cabin in Montana, word had it—went to live with a cowboy. She wrote letters to Star, telling her how much she loved her, that her loyalties had been split, but that she'd done wrong, and please could Star forgive her. Star wrote her back a concise letter that said:

Dear Janice,

Of course I forgive you. I loved you, and the good part of you will always hold a place in my heart. But how can I forget what you did?

However, if you donate money for every year of your life to the elephant sanctuary in Zambia, where I was lucky enough to spend time, then I will see you truly care and mean what you say. Elephants never forget, either, so if you do this good deed for them, then we'll be even.

Star

And that's what Star did with her Hancock Park mansion. She donated the proceeds of the sale to the elephant sanctuary, where Mindy continues to work with David.

And me? Well, it's great not having to go to SAA meetings anymore. And yeah, I know I'm still a sex addict, but when there's only one other person involved?

I think that's fair game.

21
Star

I T WAS FEBRUARY ALREADY, and my life just kept getting better and better. Well, I decided that was fair enough—I was owed that much. I mean, how could it have gotten worse? Someone up there was finally rooting for me to be happy.

Jake? Yeah, well, it scared me how much I was still so crazy about him. To compensate for my too-in-love emotions, I feigned disinterest in marriage. Sure I wanted for us to get married, but I was dealing with *Jake Wild* here. I enjoyed playing hard to get, and I knew the machinations of a man like him. A man who'd had it all handed to him on a platter: money, work, and women. His good looks, his natural talent, his family connections made it all too easy for him. His finger-snapping all those years—having women drooling and dropping their panties for him—had made him integrally pretty cocky. I needed to keep that cockiness in check.

Three days before the Oscar ceremony, I went for a check-up with my gynecologist, having had a suspicion that something was awry, but not sure because I had been so busy with rehearsals for the play we were doing in London, that I hadn't been clocking my periods.

Yup, I was pregnant. Six weeks. You couldn't tell. Although I had a feeling something was different when my breasts felt swollen twenty-four hours a day.

But I wasn't going to tell Jake. Not yet. I figured that if either, or both of us, lost out winning an Oscar—which was very likely given our strong competition—then telling him I was pregnant would be a great consolation prize.

THE BIG DAY was finally here!

I had been with Hair and Makeup since this morning, being primped and preened for this evening: The *Oscars.* This was my moment; a moment, I realized, I may never, ever experience again. But like all incredible times in your life, there is a surreal quality, which makes you feel as if you are floating on air. No drug I had ever taken (except for the Sex-with-Jake Elixir) had gotten me as high as I was now.

I had designed my own Oscar gown, after so many million-dollar contracts being offered to me that "choice-panic" set in. Besides, the idea of being "owned" by a fashion designer didn't appeal to me. I didn't want anyone dictating what I wore, no matter how much they paid me. For the first time I was dressing up for *me,* not a part I was playing, although I had to admit being "Star Davis" was a little different than Diane Davis, whom I had enjoyed immensely on my world travels.

So, after much deliberation, I opted to do my own design, which turned out exquisitely: a spaghetti-strapped long gown, cut low at the front and even lower at the back, reaching all the way down to the swell of my butt. The dress was white with thousands of little rhinestone stars hand-sewn all over it. A princess's gown, and yes, it was a Cinderella-goes-to-the-ball gown. No necklace— the stars were my jewelry, except for a matching platinum bracelet set with diamond stars that Jake had given me. In fact, it was the bracelet that inspired my design.

My shoes were high, strappy sandals with star rhinestones, custom-made by Manolo Blahnik, just for me. My hair was back to being long and blond again. It was swept up in a swirly chignon, with curly tendrils set strategically around my face. My makeup was pretty simple—but my favorite makeup artist had waved her magic wand on my head, her stardust sprinkling itself all over me, so my blue eyes shone like jewels. How she did that, I had no idea, but she was a genius. My secret weapon. My lips looked even fuller than normal, although to the naked eye it appeared as if I only wore a touch of gloss, and my cheekbones rivaled Angelina's. My skin glowed and I looked every inch the movie star.

After all, that *was* my job.

I had done the red carpet before, but this year was different. I was probably the most famous, or infamous, actor there. Not only because of my nomination for *Skye's The Limit*, but for the kidnapping, which people still held a fascination for, even nearly a year and a half later. Leo's death, the Stockholm Syndrome accusations, my brother, the revelation about Janice, the is-she-or-isn't-she? with Jake, the whole shebang, still had them all talking, pontificating, writing articles, et cetera et cetera.

The flashbulbs were blinding. The weird thing was that—as well as the fans—when we approached the intersection of Hollywood and Highland, there were some Jesus freak picketers wielding banners about burning in Hell; as if actors cornered the market on bad behavior. It made me think: the squeaky door gets the oil—or whatever that expression is—we were the ones who got noticed as being bad, or too wealthy, or too whatever, simply because we were in the limelight.

Jake and I held hands as we slowly made our way to the theatre. It took us nearly and hour with all the interviews and photos. Photographers were screaming, "Over here," and "No, over here!" The noise was deafening.

I wanted to chat to several of my friends, but they were in "movie-star" mode too. We all had to be kings and queens for tonight. Our job was to dazzle, let people all over the globe remember that Cinderella does get to go to the ball, and that the American Dream is still alive and well.

After we got inside, I sat in my seat, trying to look composed, as if being nominated alongside four other incredible actresses was the most normal thing in the world. All of us had given performances of our lifetime . . . Gwyneth, Halle, Goldie, Reese, and me . . . . sweat, tears, and certainly in my case, blood. Meryl had been nominated in the best supporting actress category. I was relieved because she wasn't competition, although the truth was that vying for the Oscar— with the other talent stacked up against me—was a very long shot. At least, in my humble opinion. Jake was convinced I'd win, but I knew he was biased.

Jake leaned over and whispered in my ear, "I forgot to say, with all the commotion earlier, you look beautiful, Star."

"You too," I whispered back, as I kept half an eye on the dancers on the stage. "You're the most dapper, debonair man here."

The evening was unfolding so quickly—a haze of beautiful designer gowns, jewels, smiles, songs, and speeches galore. Meryl won for Best Actress in a Supporting Role. I had to muster all my strength not to shed a tear. My makeup would be in ruins. I sat there, stoically, my Barbie feet taking a rest from my high heels; my dress positioned so all the tiny, hand-sewn rhinestone stars were not compromised.

The Chevaliers sat on one side of me. Pearl had also been nominated, with the other producers, in the Best Picture category for *Skye's The Limit*. She was wearing Zang Toi, the Malaysian designer who did her stunning wedding gown (I saw photos). She wore a black couture silk faille strapless gown, with a front slit, revealing some leg. It was sprinkled with ivory-colored sequins and beads. Around her elegant, long neck she wore a choker, also hand-beaded, set atop a medallion of lace. Her shoes were even higher than mine and we had been quietly groaning at each other all evening. "Did you see Glenn earlier?" she had said just before we sat down. "She flashed me her secret in the Green Room. She wears granny shoes but her dress is so long nobody can tell." I had laughed, wondering if after so many years as a Hollywood veteran as Glenn Close was, I too, would one day be at the Oscars in comfort shoes.

I nudged Pearl, whom I noticed in my peripheral vision was holding hands with Alexandre. I hoped that Jake and I would remain that in love after three kids. "Are you nervous," I whispered.

"I would be if I could breathe," she quipped. Another Hollywood costume trick: all the women here tonight (except me as I didn't want to hurt the little being inside me)—however thin—were strapped in with invisible corset-like contraptions: Spanx, fake cleavages, hoisted butts, imperceptibly engineered in ways that defied gravity and the human body—all to make each star and would-be star a specimen of perfection, to be envied and admired by millions. We all knew that everyone—

when they got home—would be squeezing out of their gorgeous outfits and slipping into tracksuits, and shoveling pizza down their gobs. Nobody, of course, had had time to eat, mostly for fear of ruining their makeup or dribbling something on their gowns.

Oh, Hollywood, my darling, what a charlatan you are!

Jake was sitting on my other side. I clasped his hand and flicked my eyes at him. He looked ravishing in his black tux. His hair was a little unruly—hadn't had time for a haircut. I knew he was nervous, although he hadn't let on. This was *it* for him. His chance to prove to the world—and his Hollywood royalty family—that he was in the big league. That his talent was equal to theirs, if not more so. And that he had the right to stick his flag at the summit of the mountain.

The next category coming up was Best Director. Jake had been nominated for *Skye's The Limit*. I felt as nervous, on his behalf, as I was for myself.

That, I told myself, is what happens when you really love someone: their feelings are your feelings, your heartbeat theirs.

PRODUCTION
Shining Star

DIRECTOR
Jake Wild

DATE
March

SCENE
The Oscars

TAKE
22

CAMERA
Jake Wild

WHEN MY UNCLE opened the envelope and called my name out as the winner for Best Achievement in Directing for *Skye's The Limit*, my first thought was, *What he's doing has to be illegal.* I was convinced that Marty or Sean must have won, and my uncle was pulling a fast one.

But the clapping began, and I had no choice but to rise from my seat. I gave Star a quick kiss, still stunned that my name had been chosen by the Academy. Then, standing on a stage before my peers, before my father, uncle, and grandfather, I began my speech. I did the usual thanking—

everyone in Christendom it seemed—I amazed myself because I did remember everybody's names. Then I said, holding the Oscar high so the audience could see:

"I would like to share this award with two people. One of whom, sadly, cannot be with us today, but because of him I learned patience and humility. Patience, to know that it's okay to have to wait for something, or in my case, someone. Humility to know that when you are a loser, it's alright. You can't win every time. And that from 'losing' you grow, learn, and ultimately heal, and that real love isn't about conquest or getting what you want, but about giving. This person once said to me, 'Jake, don't sweat it, what's yours will come to you,' and he was right."

I held the Oscar high above my head and said, "Leo, this is for you.

"The other person with whom I want to share this Oscar is my leading lady, Star Davis."

I saw her in the audience, but only just—the lights were pretty blinding—and I gazed at her glittery white outline.

"You, Star, are my leading lady in every sense

of the word. Everyone in this room knows about your extraordinary talent, your tangible, magical quality that you bring to each role, but what people perhaps don't know is your kindness, your collaborative nature, your humility when concerning your craft. And most importantly, the unfathomable depth of your heart. You taught me what it is to see. Not just on the surface, but within. To dig into a human's soul, even an animal's soul.

"Not only are you my friend, but you are an inventive genius. You created an unforgettable portrait of a murderess, sure to haunt viewers for decades to come. I salute you, my shining star: Star Davis."

I paused, surveying the audience in front of me, imagining the millions of viewers watching this show on their TV screens; some in remote, third world countries, others from the safety of their plush living rooms—all eyes on me. What I was about to do—to my knowledge—had never, since the Academy Awards began in 1929, ever been done before.

I was about to make history.

I said, trying to keep my voice from trembling, "And Star, while I'm up here tonight, in front of the world, I would like to ask you one simple question—which you don't have to answer straight away:

"Will you be my wife?"

There was an awkward hush—you could hear a pin drop, and then, after several seconds that seemed like a lifetime, the audience burst into a riotous roar of clapping. The music from *Skye's The Limit* recommenced, and Star rose to her feet and made her way to the stage, her glittering, starry gown trailing behind her. Time almost stood still—a thousand years—in slow motion—but beautiful because I treasured every split second that I had to patiently wait, as she made each small step toward me. But I was also trembling in my tuxedo: this proposal was one of many—I prayed that she'd finally accept.

But I also feared that I could fall flat on my face. She was a stubborn woman. Was I about to be humiliated in front of forty-three million people?

She walked up the steps carefully, gathering the

train of her gown in her hand, and glided toward me. She kissed me lightly on the lips, grinned at me, then turned to survey the audience. My heart was pounding a million miles an hour, thumping through my tux. She spoke to me, and also to the audience, when she said:

"If Jake Wild wants to marry a serial killer, be it on his own *head*."

The audience laughed on cue, understanding her *double-entendre*.

Star winked at me, and continued, "Yes, Jake, I *will* be your wife."

I fumbled in my pocket and took out the ring I'd had made for her: a huge, diamond star. The diamonds that made it up—seven of them, weighing forty carats—had been part of some vintage jewelry belonging to a countess, which I had bought at Christies. Vintage, hence, no modern-day, blood diamonds. I bent down on one knee and slipped the ring onto Star's engagement finger—holding it in place for several beats—my hands shaking with excitement and nerves. I stood up and brought her hand to my lips, kissing it, through my grin. I had won my real prize tonight:

Star.

The audience went crazy, leapt from their seats to give us a standing ovation, the sound of their clapping deafening. Ladies' jewels glittered and glimmered, catching the cameras. There was nothing like a vast room full of well-wishers— some of them people I admired immeasurably— willing us to be happy with their smiles, whoops of joy, and delighted faces.

But the person whom I revered most of all was standing inches away from me, and had just agreed to be my very own wife.

23. Star

I WAS A RIOTOUS JUMBLE of nerve cells, being held together by my beautiful dress. I felt like Jell-O, or the Wicked Witch of the West, that if someone threw a bucket of water on me, I might simply dissolve.

The Best Actress in a Leading Role category came straight after Best Director. Hardly had I settled down in my seat, still reeling from the fact that I had just accepted Jake's hand in marriage, and fiddling with my beautiful, enormous ring, when Brad, who was presenting this category, started telling the audience about why each one of us nominees was special. I hardly took in a word.

When it came to me, as he began a quick synopsis of my career and my role as Skye, I knew the cameras were zooming in on me; a notion I always felt so at home with, until this moment. All I could hear was the drumming of my heartbeat, like a whole parade of soldiers were inside my chest cavity. My own silent monologue inside my head, "I'm going to be married, Jake and I are getting married—oh yeah, and I'm pregnant too"—mingled with Brad's accolades.

My hearing joined in at the point when he was saying:

" . . . heartbreak and complexity and we're lucky that Star is still so young that we know we have a lifetime of her performances to look forward to." He turned his attention to me. "Star, the authenticity with which you played terrifying moments of brutality, nuanced with such tenderness and heart-wrenching despair, made us cry ugly tears, laugh, and pull out our hair. Your character Skye has to be one of the most complex of all time. If I had to choose whom to have dinner with: you, or Hannibal Lector—equally charming and equally devastating—it would be a close call."

At this point, the audience tittered with laughter.

"The transformation from girl next door to a complex serial killer will surely go down as one of the great cinematic performances in history. By the way, is security tight here tonight? I sure hope so, because with Meryl and Star in the auditorium, watch out folks!"

And when Brad opened the envelope and called out my name as Best Actress in a Leading Role, I thought I would have a coronary.

To this day, I truly can't remember what I said when I held that Oscar in my hand (it's heavy), except thanking everyone profusely for taking a chance on "a Cristal-drinking brat, fresh out of rehab," and saying how honored I was to be mentioned in the same breath as Gwyneth, Halle, Goldie, and Reese; lauding their talent and courage, and how inspired by their work I was, and breathlessly thanking the late Uta Hagen for her book, *Respect For Acting*, and all the genius actors I had ever had the pleasure of working with. And I culminated my speech by thanking Pearl and

Alexandre Chevalier, but most of all, Jake. And then I remembered his proposal all over again, and said something about him being "my-all-of-five-minutes-fiancé", and I could feel myself doing a Gwyneth-after-Shakespeare-In-Love-blubbing-with-emotion-meltdown, and Brad had to help me back to my seat.

I would hate to say it was the best day of my life, because I hope more times like that are yet to come.

But boy, what a night!

PRODUCTION
Shining Star
DIRECTOR
Jake Wild
DATE
Future
SCENE
Jake's Epilogue
TAKE
24
CAMERA
Jake Wild

"AND CUT!" I say. "That was perfect sweetheart. Just perfect."

"I want to do another take," she demands, her voice strong, shaking her blond locks in defiance.

"We don't need to darling, it's in the can—we're good."

"I can do better."

I observe my four-year-old with exasperation. How is it possible that such a little being has me—not only singing for my supper—but wrapped around her pinkie finger?

"Actually, Jake, there's a hair in the gate, we

need to go again." It's Paul, my cameraman. He shrugs. "Hero's right."

"See," Hero sings. "I told you so."

I narrow my eyes at Paul. Hmm . . . suspicious. Hero has him under her spell. In fact, she has the entire cast and crew completely delighted with her.

Hero. My daughter. Named after one of Shakespeare's heroines in *Much Ado About Nothing*. An apt name for her, as, yes, she does have us running around, often for nothing.

Hero decided, at the ripe young age of three and three-quarters that she wanted—and deserved—a little gold man called Oscar to hang out with her in her playroom. "But you have to earn him," I explained. "He can't be bought or traded, not even on ebay," Star told her, "Oscar has to be *won*." So that's when little Hero made it her mission in life to be an actress. And namely, an Oscar-winning actress.

Not only do I have to contend with my tyrant of a daughter, but Fierces's daughter too. Yes, she is also starring in this movie we're making, *Dog's Don't Cry*.

Fierce escaped one evening and went acourting. He impregnated a Springer Spaniel, and their unusual looking offspring—a Rhodesian Ridgeback/Spaniel long-eared mutt, with insane amounts of energy—is now the toast of Hollywood after intensive acting lessons with an animal trainer who specializes in big cats.

"We need Bobby!" the AD shouts, and into the walkie-talkie: "Bobby on set please. I repeat, Bobby on set."

Someone replies, "She's in Hair and Makeup being groomed."

I laugh. This is now my life. Sex-addict Jake Wild's every move is being run by dogs and children.

Star's Epilogue

THE RHYTHMN OF the hammock being pushed back and forth by little Hero, mixed with the lapping of the Malibu ocean waves, is soporific. The warm salty breeze sailing in from the beach that is our front yard is just what I need after a long day. This is a job my little daughter takes very seriously: Helping Mommy Relax.

"Tell me about your day, sweetheart," I say. "Did Daddy behave himself?"

"Pretty much. Bobby pushed him over."

I giggle. "Well yes, Daddy is a bit of a pushover these days, but that's just how it should be. We girls need to keep our men under control."

I look at my four-year-old to see if she's caught my irony and she has. She winks at me, albeit with both eyes at the same time—she's still learning that trick. I pull her onto the hammock with me and nuzzle my face in her hair. How could anyone be so delicious? We have a lovely long cuddle as I breathe her in. My life. My love. How can so much savvy and kick-ass attitude be packed into such a tiny body?

"Like mother, like daughter," a voice says, reading my thoughts.

I look over. It's Jake, a whiskey in his hand, a soft crinkle at the edge of his eyes, and the sparkle in his irises showing amusement, but his lips giving nothing away. It's great to see how he's now able to enjoy the odd evening drink without going overboard. He has mellowed. In some ways. In others, not.

"I do believe it's bedtime sweetie."

"Me or Hero?" I ask.

"Hero. I'm going to read her a story, and as for you, Mrs. Wild, I'll deal with *you* afterwards." No smile, no joke. I know what he has in mind for me.

"OH GOD," I SAY, the mask on my eyes making every tiny nuance of sound sharper, more acute.

"But you're aware you deserve this; you realize you've been disobedient," he reprimands me, no humor in his voice.

"I know," I agree.

"So you can imagine what that means."

"Yes," I whisper.

I can hear his footsteps pace agitatedly around me, but I'm unable to move. I'm splayed out like a starfish (no pun intended), my wrists cuffed, one on either side, to the bedposts. The cuffs are padded—there'll be no bruising, but still, I have zero control. My ankles he's tied with silk scarves, also to the posts, at the bottom of the bed. I had no idea when the four-poster arrived that it would change the course of our sex-life:

We both have a new addiction.

I sense the tassels brush up and down me, circling my hard nipples, stroking softly down the center of my torso; no hurry, just a soft, slow, deliberate tease. I can feel the wetness build inside me. I wonder where he'll go next. Or what he'll do next. He's always unpredictable. The tassels tickle—the languid, unhurried strokes barely touch my sensitive skin. On my calf now and up one leg, up, up, then between my thighs. Trailing over my clit. Suddenly there's a stinging strike right at my opening.

"Aahh," I squeal out.

"That's for being so bossy," Jake murmurs.

I writhe on the linen sheets, wishing I could claw them—grab something—but I'm bound. Totally at his mercy. I'm tingling all over, throbbing, wanting more, but I can't see what's coming next with the blindfold on. Then the mattress dips and Jake is getting on the bed. I want to touch him but can't. He has his legs on either side of my hips.

He thrusts his cock into me in one punctuated stroke. I cry out, glad that Hero's room is at the other end of the house.

But as unexpectedly as he shoves it into me, he withdraws, moves himself off me, and I'm left bereft and panting. "Please," I say.

"You need to earn it, baby."

"How?"

The tassel torture starts again. Up past my belly button, then circling around each breast but not touching my nipples. "Please."

"Please what, Star?"

"I need you to fuck me. I need to come."

The tassel trails up to my shoulders, softly brushing from one side to the other. It disappears for what seems like half a minute, and my heart starts racing, but the flogger comes down with a thwack on my clit. It stings like hell for a second, but then I feel that heavy throb again.

"Oh, God," I moan. I want to laugh at the absurdity of it all. I know what Jake has been doing all day: running around in circles after an unruly dog. Last week, they were shooting a scene where Bobby had to turn on the bathtub faucet with her paw and mayhem ensued. Filming animals and children has not been easy for him.

He often tells me that his mind wanders to me, to this, to fucking me when he's at work, and I tease him, telling him I have "business" meetings with hot young actors I'm "auditioning" for our next project. Jake knows I'm lying, but it gets him all worked up. Gets him hard. Jealousy is his aphrodisiac. Sometimes a car arrives to take me to the set midday so he can fuck me in between takes. Other times he unexpectedly comes home. We made a deal not to both work at the same time unless it's both of us on one movie. He can't bear to be apart from me.

I say, "That new young actor, what's his name, the buffed-up one that girls wet their panties over? The one you met for the role of Stevie?"

The tassel stops mid-tease. "Sean O' Connor, what about him?"

"Pearl thinks he'd be a good leading man for me and you should hire him."

"Does she now."

I feel his knees dig back into the mattress either side of my shoulders. "Stop talking nonsense and suck my cock. Open that smart mouth of yours. Now."

I do as I'm directed, my tongue finding his silky wide crest as he pushes his huge erection deep into my mouth. He groans. "Oh fuck baby, you drive me crazy. You're fucking gorgeous. I'm so in love with you."

I wrap my lips tightly around his hardness, creating suction as he fucks my mouth slowly. His moans of pleasure have me wetting up even more. I love that I can get my man so turned on. But then he takes his cock away. *What's happening?* He's gone again. But I feel the stroke of it once more, the soft crown of his dick teasing each of my nipples in turn as he tantalizes my teats with his tip. He loves coming on my tits; is that what he has in mind?

I'm writhing beneath the bed, my arms straining against the handcuffs, my hips bucking up at him. Then his lips are on my mouth, his tongue inside—he's groaning and breathing sex. My ankles are still tied. His mouth trails down to my throat, my breasts, kissing, nibbling, nipping, sucking. His fingers slip into my wet heat and he growls in appreciation of how soaked I am. He takes his fingers out—a languid tease—and I hear him pop them into his mouth.

"Fuck, your taste gets me . . . . so. Fucking. Hard."

He moves away from me again and I feel one ankle being untied, then the other. Relief; I can bend my knees. He gathers my legs, folds them into me so my knees are resting on my stomach, and in one swift move thrusts himself inside me. Hard. He pulls out very slowly, nearly all the way and repeats his brand of torture, ramming into me ruthlessly on a growl. He keeps up this rhythm, each time I rise my hips to meet him, the only movement allowed to me.

This time, he's the one to come first, but his guttural groans of pleasure and his thick cock expanding inside me, and pushing against my walls, is all it takes for me to start coming too, my climax hard-earned as it pulses through me in powerful spasms. I grip his cock with my inner muscles and he moves gently inside me, our last ripples of pleasure weakening both of us.

"I love it when you do that," he says.

"What?"

"Cling onto me with your pussy, grasping it like that. Like you never, ever want to let me go."

"I don't."

"How can I be sure?"

"You can't," I tease, "that's why you're still in love with me."

"You're incorrigible, Star."

"Un-cuff me now, and un-blindfold me."

He's still inside me, his lips on my mouth, and says, "I don't know about that, I quite like you helpless like this."

"Untie me, Wild."

He chuckles. "What's in it for me?"

"I'll tell you a secret."

Jake carefully pulls out of me, and giving me a kiss on the nose, clambers over me, finds the key, and unlocks each handcuff. I rip off my blindfold and burst out laughing. He's standing there, a bemused look on his gorgeous face; the face of a just-fucked man in his element. His eyes still half-mast and lusty.

"What's so funny?" he says.

"Us."

"Why?"

"Because we're such a nutty pair. We certainly met our match."

"And that match started a fire."

"But we have it under control, don't we? I mean it's sort of smoldering now. The fire. Hot, but smoldering." I rub my wrists and grin at him, wondering if we *do* have things under control. Our life is always one big improvisation . . . we never know what will happen next. We flew to Vegas, for instance, straight after the Vanity Fair party, after the Oscars. Pearl flew us there in her HookedUp jet. And she and Alexandre were our witnesses. We got married in a tacky chapel with an Elvis minister. It was kitsch, over-the-top. But so exciting. I didn't even need to change my white, star-spangled Oscar gown; it was perfect.

Life for us is always unexpected. Well, what can you expect from a couple of Hollywood misfits with more money than sense?

I sigh, my gaze still connected with my husband's smiling eyes. I'm too tired to leave the bed.

"So what's that secret you promised to tell me?" he asks.

I lay my hand on my belly. "I'm pregnant. We have another Wild Child on the way. This time, a boy. I was thinking of naming him Leo, what do you think?"

"I think that's perfect," he said, his eyes glimmering with happiness. "Just perfect."

THE END

Thank you so much for choosing **_Shining Star_** to be part of your library and I hope you enjoyed reading it as much as I enjoyed writing it. If you loved this book and have a minute please write a quick review. It helps authors so much. I am thrilled that you chose my book to be part of your busy life and hope to be re-invited to your bookshelf with my next release.

If you haven't read my other books I would love you to give them a try. The Pearl Series is a set of five, full-length erotic romance novels. I have also written a suspense novel, _Stolen Grace_.

The Pearl Trilogy

(all three books in one big volume)

Shades of Pearl

Shadows of Pearl

Shimmers of Pearl

Pearl

Belle Pearl

Join me on Facebook

(facebook.com/AuthorArianneRichmonde)

Join me on Twitter

(@A_Richmonde)

For more information about me, visit my website

(www.ariannerichmonde.com).

If you would like to email me:

ariannerichmonde@gmail.com

Made in the USA
Middletown, DE
13 January 2017